Strike Three!

The Chip Hilton Sports Series

For more information on
Chip Hilton-related activities and to correspond
with other Chip fans, check the Internet at
www.chiphilton.com

Chip Hilton Sports Series
#3

Strike Three!

Coach Clair Bee
Updated by Randall and Cynthia Bee Farley

BROADMAN
& HOLMAN
PUBLISHERS

Nashville, Tennessee

0-8054-1816-4

Published by Broadman & Holman Publishers,
Nashville, Tennessee

Subject Heading: BASEBALL—FICTION / YOUTH
Library of Congress Card Catalog Number: 98-28094

Library of Congress Cataloging-in-Publication Data
Bee, Clair.
    Strike three! / by Clair Bee ; edited by Cynthia Bee Farley
and Randall K. Farley.
      p. cm. — (Chip Hilton sports series ; v. 3)
    Updated ed. of a work published in 1949.
    Summary: When Chip Hilton learns the reason for the
animosity shown him by two other members of the baseball team,
he finds a way to overcome the problem.
    ISBN 0-8054-1816-4 (alk. paper)
    [1. Baseball—Fiction. 2. Sportsmanship—Fiction.
3. Teamwork (Sports)—Fiction.] I. Farley, Cynthia Bee, 1952– .
II. Farley, Randall K., 1952– . III. Title. IV. Series: Bee, Clair.
Chip Hilton sports series ; v. 3.

PZ7.B38196St   1998
[Fic]—dc21   98-28094
                                                     CIP
                                                     AC

4 5 6 7 04 03 02 01

DAVE LOWE
PATRIOT, STUDENT, ATHLETE

HE GAVE ALL HE HAD FOR HIS COUNTRY AND HIS TEAM.

Dave Lowe was the regular varsity catcher for the
Long Island University baseball team for three years.
He lost his life flying over Germany during World War II.

COACH CLAIR BEE, 1949

MARLO TERMINI
PROFESSOR, COACH, MENTOR

A life dedicated to America's young people
and the most enthusiastic of voices!
You taught us the greatest gifts are service and love.

Clair Bee's friend and ours.

RANDY AND CINDY FARLEY, 1998

Contents

CONTENTS

Foreword

I CAN remember that in the early and midfifties when I was in junior high and high school, there was nothing more exciting, outside of actually playing a game, than reading one of the books from Coach Bee's Chip Hilton series. He wrote twenty-three books in all, and I bought and read each one of them during my student days. His books were about the three sports that I played—football, basketball, and baseball—and had the kind of characters in them that every young boy wanted to imagine that he was or could become.

No one person has ever contributed more to the game of basketball in the development of the fundamental skills, tactics, and strategies of the game than Clair Bee during his fifty years as a teacher of the sport. I strongly believe that the same can be said of his authorship of the Chip Hilton series.

STRIKE THREE!

The enjoyment that a young athlete can get from reading the Chip Hilton series is just as great today as it was for me more than forty years ago. The lessons that Clair Bee teaches through Chip Hilton and his exploits are the most meaningful and priceless examples of what is right and fair about life that I have ever read. I have the entire series in a glass case in my library at home. I spend a lot of hours browsing through those twenty-three books.

As a coach, I will always be indebted to Clair Bee for the many hours he spent helping me learn about the game of basketball. As a person, I owe an even greater debt to him for providing me with the most memorable reading of my youth through his series on Chip Hilton.

Bob Knight
HEAD BASKETBALL COACH, INDIANA UNIVERSITY

DURING THE summer of 1959 at the New York Military Academy, not only did I stare at the painting of the fictional folk hero—Chip Hilton—that was on the wall behind Coach Bee's dining room table, but I had the opportunity to read some of the Chip Hilton series. The books were extremely interesting and well written, using sports as a vehicle to build character. No one did that better than Clair Bee (although John R. Tunis came close). By that time, Bee's Chip Hilton books had become a classic series for youngsters. While Coach Bee was well known as one of the greatest coaches of all time, due to his strategy and competitiveness, I believe he thought he could help society and young people most by writing this

FOREWORD

series. In his eyes, it was his "calling" in the years following his college and professional coaching career.

From 1959 until his death, I visited with Coach Bee frequently at the New York Military Academy and at Kutsher's Sport Academy, which he directed. He certainly touched my life as a special friend. Not only does he still rank at the top of his profession as a basketball coach, but he now regains the peak as a writer of sports fiction. I am delighted the Chip Hilton Sports series has been redone to make it more appropriate for athletics today, without losing the deeper meaning of defining character. I encourage everyone to give these books as gifts to other young athletes so that Coach Bee's brilliant method of making sports come to life and of building character will continue.

Dean E. Smith
HEAD COACH (RETIRED), MEN'S BASKETBALL,
UNIVERSITY OF NORTH CAROLINA AT CHAPEL HILL

IT'S SOMETIMES difficult to figure out why we became who we became. Was it an influential teacher who steered you toward biology? A beloved grandparent who turned you into a machinist? A motorcycle accident that forced you into accounting?

All I know is that in my case the Chip Hilton books had something—no, a lot—to do with my becoming a sports journalist. At the very least, the books got me to sit down and read when others of my generation were watching television or otherwise goofing off; at most, they taught me many of life's lessons, about sports and sportsmanship, about coaches and coaching, about winning and losing.

Since writing and selling to *Sports Illustrated* a piece about Clair Bee that appeared in 1979, I've written hundreds of other articles, many of them cover stories about famous athletes like Michael Jordan, Magic Johnson, and Larry Bird; yet I'm still known, by and large, as the "guy who wrote the Chip Hilton story." I would safely say that still, two decades later, six months do not go by that I don't receive some kind of question about Clair and Chip.

As I leafed through one of the books recently, a memory came back to me from my days as a twelve-year-old Pop Warner football player in Mays Landing, New Jersey. A friend who shared my interest in the books had just thrown an opposing quarterback for a loss in a key game. As we walked back to the huddle, he put his arm on my shoulder pads and conjuring up a Hilton gang character, whispered, "Another jarring tackle by Biggie Cohen." No matter how old you get, you never forget something like that. Thank you, Clair Bee.

Jack McCallum
SENIOR WRITER, *SPORTS ILLUSTRATED*

CHAPTER 1

Switch Hitter

WILLIAM "CHIP" HILTON was standing on deck swinging three bats. His long arms curled the bats back over his left shoulder in a free, easy motion and then whistled them forward in a full left-handed swing. The follow-through was so complete that it twisted the tall teenager all the way around on the spiked toes of his baseball shoes.

Chip had put more into the swing than was necessary because he was "rarin' to go!" For three long, dreary weeks, the Valley Falls High School diamond prospects had been penned indoors with Coach Henry Rockwell's baseball training drills because it had rained every day. Chip and everyone else were restless with the indoor drills and irritated with the weather. Baseball was an outdoor game! Now at last they were outside where they belonged.

Chip looked up at the bright, blue sky and could hardly resist the urge to yell at the top of his voice. Then he felt a little pull along the muscles and tendons of his

STRIKE THREE!

left leg, and he dropped back on his heels and looked down at the bandaged ankle. It was still stiff and tight.

S-M-A-C-K! The ball struck the catcher's big mitt.

Chip shifted his eyes toward the catcher's box and the player who had just caught the pitch from the mound. Carl Carey was grinning as he rifled the ball back to Nick Trullo.

"Atta boy, Nick," Carl yelled, "burn 'em in!"

Chip studied the stocky receiver carefully. Carey had all the characteristics of a catcher. He was compactly built and quick on his feet. Once again, Chip stretched his newly mended left ankle. Perhaps the ankle wouldn't hold up through the season; maybe it would mean Chip Hilton wouldn't be needed as the first-string catcher. Well, time would take care of that. But right *now,* Chip Hilton was the Big Reds' number-one receiver, and Carl Carey was going to have a rough time taking over.

"All right, Hilton," Rockwell shouted, "let's go!"

Chip stepped up to the first-base side of the plate, tugged his batting helmet a little farther down over his blond, short-cropped hair, and carefully eyed the tall, broad-shouldered southpaw on the mound.

Trullo began his windup and then blazed a fast one straight for Hilton's head. Chip fell away from the ball and landed in the dirt. It was a clumsy fall, and the tall batter's face was burning as he slowly got to his feet. He picked up the bat and gave Trullo a long, questioning look.

Carl Carey chuckled as he returned the ball to Trullo. "What's the matter, Hilton?" he taunted. "Don't you like a high, fast one?"

Hilton ignored Carey completely. Standing out of the batter's box, he slowly fixed his helmet on his head and then walked around behind the smiling catcher to the other side of the plate. He hitched his waistband, yanked his cap down over his left eye, and stepped into the box. "Now bean me," he muttered.

Over in front of the home dugout, Coach Henry Rockwell, known by everyone in Valley Falls and throughout the state as the "Rock," thoughtfully studied the tall, gray-eyed batter. "Switch hitting," he said softly, half to himself and half to the two men standing on either side of him. "Using his head—"

Chet Stewart, the smaller of Rockwell's two assistants, nodded. "Sure," he agreed, "maybe figures he can watch that fast one a little more closely. Beanballs sometimes give a fellow a headache."

Rockwell smiled. "Now, Chet," he said, "Trullo probably doesn't know what a beanball is. Even if he does, he wouldn't use it deliberately. I'd throw him right off the squad! He knows that."

Bill Thomas, the big, broad-shouldered assistant coach on Rockwell's left, shuffled uneasily. "Maybe Trullo's just a little wild," he suggested quietly. "It's the first day out, you know. First time he's been on the mound."

"And maybe there's more to it than wildness!" Stewart remarked grimly.

Thomas studied Stewart's grim expression. "Like what?" he asked.

"A little thing like a buddy trying to beat someone out of a job," Stewart said dryly.

Rockwell was thinking about Nick Trullo and Valley Falls's dire need for a pitcher. The previous year, the Big Reds had been blessed with two fine hurlers, Tim Murphy and Rick Hanson. But both had graduated, and now Rockwell was without an experienced pitcher, and the first game was a little more than two weeks away.

"Trullo *has* to be it!" he mused. "That is, if he has any control at all. He's the only thrower there is on *this* team!"

STRIKE THREE!

In the batter's box, Chip Hilton watched the intent face of Nick Trullo. The big, swarthy boy might dust him off again, but Chip wasn't about to get hit or be forced to sprawl on the ground again.

Trullo drove a high pitch toward the plate. The spinning ball broke sharply six feet in front of Hilton and shot toward his head. But this time, Chip was ready. He pulled his head back just enough, grinned, and rapped the plate with his bat.

"What's the matter, Nick?" he called. "Can't you find the plate? No control?"

"His control's all right," growled Carey. "He's throwin' 'em right where I want 'em!"

Again, Chip ignored Carey and tapped the plate with his bat. "There's the spot, Nick. Afraid to put it over?" he bantered.

The big left-hander's eyes narrowed dangerously, and he wound up and blazed the ball at Hilton's head again. Chip ducked a bit and then caught the speeding ball in his bare hand. He laughed as he rolled the ball back on the ground toward the angry pitcher.

"Aw, come on, Nick," he chided. "Is that the best you've got? Put something on it! Throw it hard once!"

Trullo blazed another one at Chip. This time the ball was in the dirt. Chip kicked it with his foot as the ball bounced over the plate.

Carl Carey's flushed face matched Trullo's as he chased the ball and whipped it back to the mound. "Strike the star out, Nick," he called.

"Hold it!" Coach Rockwell strode out to the plate. "What's going on here?" He motioned to Trullo and waited silently as the boy walked slowly toward the plate.

"This is supposed to be hitting practice, Trullo," he said quietly, "not pitching practice. I want straight pitches—over the plate! Understand?"

Trullo nodded. "I understand, Coach," he said.

"OK. Go back out there and throw 'em over. Only straight stuff!"

Trullo pitched carefully to Chip, but not carefully enough. Chip met each pitch over the plate between his knees and his shoulders with a smooth swing, and the ball took off for clean, solid hits.

Major-league catchers are good hitters and have good eyes. Chip had caught every game for Valley Falls the year before, and he had developed the skill of following the ball right up to the split second when it met the bat.

The ball came in from Trullo, and Chip gave it a full rip. C-R-A-C-K! The ball sailed in a whistling arc far out into center field and bounded crazily up against the scoreboard. Soapy Smith tore after the speeding pellet with Ted Williams in hot pursuit. Soapy recovered the ball as it hit the turf, dodged Williams, set himself, and threw it all the way from center field to home plate on the fly. As the tremendous heave came arching in from center field, Chris Badger was just stooping to pick up a bat. Plop! The ball landed right behind him. Everybody laughed when Badger looked up in surprise. Chris whirled around and shook his fist at the grinning Soapy.

Chip's eyes shifted from one grinning face to another. Yes, Chris and Cody Collins had come around all right. The old trouble of last fall's football season was forgotten. It was great to play on a *team*.

Then Hilton's eyes went back to the mound. Nick Trullo stood there, not even bothering to hide the scorn and anger on his face. Behind him, Carl Carey muttered something about grandstand hitting. Trullo had played regular center on the varsity football squad and had sided with Badger and Collins in the division that had almost wrecked the team. Even after Chris and Cody had put aside their differences, Nick had remained aloof. Now that his buddy, Carl Carey, was vying for Chip's job as regular catcher, Trullo seemed more ill-tempered than ever.

Chip's mind went back to the scene in the locker room that afternoon when they were dressing for practice. Chip, Speed Morris, and Biggie Cohen had been discussing the pitching situation. It was too bad, Chip had said, that both of last year's strong pitchers had graduated in the same year. Trullo, overhearing Chip's thoughtless remark, had startled everyone by suddenly breaking into the conversation.

"They *must* have been good if you were the regular catcher, Hilton!"

Chip had been perplexed by the sudden bitterness in Nick's voice but had dismissed the remark. He hadn't known much about Trullo's ability then. He knew now Nick Trullo did have the makings of a good pitcher, even though his lack of control over his temper was obvious in his lack of control on the mound. He had plenty on the ball and a world of speed. With the right catcher . . . .

Chip could understand why one South-Sider stuck by another; why Trullo so openly wanted his friend to win the backstop job. That was OK, but an athlete should earn his job on his own merits.

In front of the dugout, Rockwell and his two assistants were discussing the personnel of the team. Back from the previous year were Chip Hilton, the regular catcher; Speed Morris, star shortstop; Biggie Cohen, left-handed first baseman and a powerhouse at the plate; Ted Williams, a strong-hitting outfielder; and several reserves: Soapy Smith, Red Schwartz, and Mike Rodriguez.

Some of the newcomers looked good. Cody Collins, a regular pepperbox, was already tabbed as the most likely prospect for the second-base job. Chris Badger, star full-back from last year's championship football team, had everything third base, the hot corner, needed—a strong, accurate arm, courage, and speed. It looked as though the infield was all set. But pitching was something else; Murphy and Hanson would be hard to replace.

Rockwell nodded toward Hilton and the group. "Looks like the football feud between the West- and South-Siders is all cleared up," he said.

"I wouldn't be too sure," Chet Stewart said dryly. He gestured toward Trullo and Carey. "Personally, I think those two spell trouble."

"Maybe not," Bill Thomas said softly. "Anyway, I sure hope not! Trullo looks to me like the only pitcher we may have on this ball club. And so far, the Carey kid handles the receiver's duties OK. A team never has too many catchers." He nodded his head in agreement as Rockwell added, "Nor too many pitchers!"

Rockwell ended the discussion by summoning everyone to home plate. Two deep lines between his penetrating black eyes were pulled close together in a frown. The players sensed his mood instantly. They watched him silently as he kicked his spikes across the clay in front of the plate and glared at Soapy Smith.

Rockwell was dressed in an old, faded baseball uniform that had shrunk from too many washings until it fitted him like paper on a wall. But the snug fit merely accentuated the strength in his powerful frame. The Rock stood five feet, ten inches in his stocking feet, and his 180 pounds were all muscle. He was rugged all right. His black hair and agile movements belied his nearly sixty years.

He pulled his old broken-billed cap down over one eye and then let loose a torrent of words.

STRIKE THREE!

"The first day out on the field and some grade school bush leaguer—" He paused and glared around the circle of faces until he met Soapy Smith's eyes. "Some bush leaguer like you, Smith, tries to throw his arm away by showing how he can rifle a ball in from the outfield! Thousands of boys every year make the same mistake you just made, Smith. They want to show off! Don't warm up thoroughly and slowly, and so they throw their arms away the first couple of weeks of practice and wind up with glass arms for the rest of their lives.

"Now, all of you listen to me!" Rockwell shook a finger around the circle of intent faces. "And pay attention! I don't want to see anyone else showing off out here. The next player I see throwing his arm away will join Smith—in the bleachers!"

He turned to Soapy. "That's all for you today, Smith. See me in my office tomorrow afternoon at 3:30 sharp!"

A little later Chip took his place in line as Rockwell prepared to time the squad around the bases. When Chip's turn came, he stepped into the batter's box nearest first base. Rockwell stopped him.

"What do you think you're doing?" he asked.

"I'm going to run the bases, Coach!"

"No, you're not, young man! You'll do no running or sliding out here for another two or three weeks! We won't take any chances with that ankle!"

Chip's face flushed, and he clenched his fists in frustration as he stepped reluctantly from the box. How long was this going to last? All through basketball season he had been forced to sit on the sidelines.

Sure, the team had given him the basketball for contributing the most to the team's success in the state finals, but he hadn't earned it! It was an honor, but he didn't want honors. He wanted to play.

SWITCH HITTER

By the time Rockwell yelled, "Hit the showers," Chip was steaming. All of Speed Morris's and Biggie Cohen's efforts to snap him out of his angry mood were unsuccessful, and he hurried through his shower and quickly dressed in silence. Outside the gym, the three boys climbed into Speed's Mustang, Chip in the back and Biggie in front. Speed had painted his beloved red "pony" with new spring decorations: brilliant white stripes— Valley Falls High School colors.

After turning on the radio, Biggie turned around, looked at Chip, and broke the silence. "Look, Chip, you can't rush right into everything! You know a broken ankle isn't like a sprain. It takes time!"

"Time?" Chip snapped. "Time!" he repeated incredulously. "It's been nearly six months. Major-league players sometimes break an ankle in spring practice and get back in the lineup in six weeks! Six *weeks,* not six *months!*"

After his outburst, Chip lapsed into moody silence. Suddenly, he felt Speed's car shaking more than usual. Looking up front at Biggie, he saw the big first baseman's shoulders heaving with silent laughter.

"What's so funny?" Chip demanded.

Biggie let out a roar. He was still heaving with laughter when the red-and-white fastback pulled up in front of the Hilton home.

"If you could only see your face right now, Chip!" he gasped. "Your face is the perfect advertisement for the Sugar Bowl's special bittersweet chocolate!"

Who could stay angry with Biggie around? Chip and Speed suddenly joined their laughter with Cohen's booming roars.

"As Soapy would badly say," panted Speed with tears in his eyes, "'let joy be unrefined!'"

CHAPTER 2

Like Father— Like Son

CHIP HUNG UP the telephone and joined his mother at the dinner table. He had reached Soapy at home. He knew his friend would be worried. They agreed to meet that night at the Sugar Bowl. He wanted to save Soapy a night's sleep.

Mary Hilton's clear, gray eyes studied her tall, blond son sitting quietly across from her. Mrs. Hilton had the same shade of hair, the same eyes, and the same thin lips as her son, but there the resemblance ended. Mary Hilton was petite while Chip was tall, rangy, and broad-shouldered.

"What's the matter, son?"

Chip told his mother about that day's practice and about his leg. A bit hesitantly, he told her also about the competition behind the plate. Nick Trullo looked like the only pitcher out for the team, and he had already made it clear he wanted Carl Carey as his receiver.

"Chip, why don't you try to be friends with Nick?"

Chip explained that after practice he had asked Trullo why he was angry. Trullo had said, "Look, Hilton, I'm not angry. You're just not the kind of guy I like. As far as that's concerned, I don't like any of you West-Siders. You're all the same!"

A puzzled Chip had asked what that had to do with baseball. Trullo had sneered, "Rockwell babied you in football and basketball, and now he's babying you in baseball. Carl's a better catcher than you are, and Rockwell knows it! But he won't give him a chance because you're one of his pets. If Carl would suck up to Rockwell the way you do, he'd be a cinch for the job."

"You see, Mom," Chip said anxiously, "there wasn't anything I could say after that. I wasn't getting anywhere with him except closer to a fight."

Mary Hilton nodded her head understandingly. "I think you did all you could under the circumstances, Chip. I do wish, though, there was a way you could be friendly with those two boys. What sort of boy is Carl Carey?"

"He's OK, I guess," Chip said slowly. "I haven't had any trouble with him. 'Course, he and Nick are good friends, and I suppose he feels the same way Nick does."

"Is Carl a good catcher, Chip?"

"He looks good, Mom! He's fast on his feet, and he's got a strong build. Beside him, I look like a stick. And the way I'm moving around on my ankle, you'd think I still had the cast on!"

Mary Hilton smiled. "Coach Rockwell didn't mind having a 'stick' for a catcher last year, did he, Chip?"

"I know, Mom, but there weren't any real catchers around last year."

The corners of Mary Hilton's eyes crinkled with laughter. "Well, there must be a lot of people in this state who don't know anything about baseball then. I seem to remember several articles about a certain Valley Falls catcher who made All-State last year."

"That was last year—," Chip began, but his mom interrupted him gently.

"I'd not worry too much about it, Chip. You'll make out all right. And by the way, from where I sit, I can see a pitching rubber and a home plate out there in the backyard." Warmth radiated from Mary Hilton's eyes. "Did you say Nick Trullo was the *only* pitcher on this year's squad?"

Chip turned to look out in the backyard. Long ago his father, "Big Chip" Hilton, had converted the space into a miniature athletic field. The "Hilton Athletic Club" contained a basketball court with two regulation baskets and backboards; a set of goal posts directly against the back fence; and, running north and south, a pitching rubber with a home plate, sixty feet, six inches away.

Big Chip Hilton had worked out there almost every evening with his young son. Little Chip had developed into a fine place-kicker in football, a great shot in basketball, and a hard thrower in baseball. Chip was endowed with all the physical requisites a pitcher needed. All he lacked was experience and a variety of pitches.

Chip searched his mother's gray eyes deeply. Then he snapped his fingers. "Mom, maybe you've got something there. Why, there're only Nick Trullo and Lefty Peters out for pitching, and they're both southpaws. I can throw as hard as they can!" Chip spread the fingers of his right hand and looked at them thoughtfully. His long fingers were strong and graceful; they might have been those of a concert pianist.

Mary Hilton had noted those supple fingers long ago, but all her efforts to teach her son to play the piano hadn't gotten very far. Chip had tried hard, but the call to become an athlete was too strong.

Chip bolted from the table. "Excuse me, Mom. Where's Dad's old catcher's glove? Maybe I can get Taps to catch some!"

Later, Mary Hilton glanced at the kitchen clock and then stepped to the window overlooking the backyard Hilton Athletic Club. Chip was throwing to a tall teenager. Taps Browning and Chip had been close friends ever since the Browning family had moved next door the previous fall.

Mary Hilton was thinking of Big Chip and Little Chip, as they used to be called. In his younger days Big Chip had been a catcher, but he had always wanted Little Chip to be a pitcher, and he had coached him in pitching for years. He had dreamed of the day when his son would be a star hurler. But that had never worked out. Rockwell had been abundantly supplied with pitchers in Chip's freshman year and had planted the eager youngster on first base because of his height and long arms.

Chip had played well on first base during his freshman year. In his sophomore year, Biggie Cohen had been taken out of the outfield and placed on the initial bag, and Chip had been shifted again—behind the plate this time.

Mary Hilton's suggestion to her son was the result of a hope that Big Chip's wish might come true. When Mary Hilton had first met Bill Hilton, she had teasingly called him a bush leaguer. But Big Chip would never have been a bush leaguer. He was one of Valley Falls's all-time greats in all sports. In baseball he had been a star, and major-league scouts had waited in line with contracts.

STRIKE THREE!

Big Chip had been sorely tempted to give baseball a try as a profession after his graduation from college. But he had also dreamed of a career in ceramics and of home-town life with Mary Carson. And so professional baseball had lost a great player.

Big Chip Hilton had not lived to see his boy play on a Valley Falls High School team. An accident had taken care of that. One of the workmen in a kiln at the pottery had been piling big containers of ware, one upon the other. A bottom container was cracked, and just as Big Chip entered the kiln on an inspection tour, it gave way. Hilton had knocked the workman aside in time to save the careless man's life but had caught the whole force of the tumbling containers himself. He was crushed beneath the debris.

Through misty eyes, Mary Hilton watched her long-legged son set himself and send the ball thudding into the exact spot where Taps Browning was holding the big catcher's glove.

"He looks like a pitcher to me," she murmured. "He's tall, and certainly his arms are long enough. Little Chipper, so . . . so much like his father."

She glanced at the clock again and moved reluctantly toward the door. It was time for Chip to go to work, and she wished he could be free from the concern of helping out with the family expenses. The salary she earned at the telephone company was good but didn't stretch quite far enough with a son a few years away from entering college. Mary Hilton faithfully set aside a part of her monthly earnings toward Chip's college education.

"It's nearly seven o'clock, Chip," she called. "You'll be late!"

LIKE FATHER—LIKE SON

John Schroeder's Sugar Bowl was the favorite meeting place for Valley Falls high school students. It resembled an old-fashioned ice cream and soda fountain shop in decor. Schroeder had kept the long wooden counter with stools and had added booths and tables. Ice-cream dishes, pizza, and hamburgers were the most popular items on the Sugar Bowl menu. His newest additions included several thundering video games and an antique juke box that belted out the current top hits. He also owned the pharmacy next door but spent most of his time in the storeroom that serviced both stores. Chip had started to work for Mr. Schroeder shortly after the death of his father, and the friendship between the two had long since passed the stage of owner/employer and employee; it was more of an uncle and nephew relationship.

Once at the Sugar Bowl, Chip went directly to the storeroom, evading Petey Jackson, Valley Falls's fountain manager and self-proclaimed sports guru. Petey called out to Chip, "Come see something," but Chip had another problem to solve, and he wasn't interested right now in anything Petey Jackson might have in the way of a trick, joke, or puzzle.

John Schroeder, seated at his large, antique desk in the corner, looked up as Chip entered. "Hello, Chipper," he greeted. "How was practice today?"

"Pretty good, Mr. Schroeder."

"How was old Gibraltar?"

Chip smiled. "Oh, you know the coach, Mr. Schroeder. He's *always* the same. Do you mind if I go up to see Doc Jones a minute?"

"Of course not, Chip. But he isn't due in his office until eight o'clock."

John Schroeder's brown eyes suddenly sobered. "What's the trouble, Chip?" he asked.

"Oh, nothing much. I . . . I just wanted Doc to look at my ankle."

Chip turned away and began his work while his employer resumed his writing at the desk. John Schroeder knew Chip well; he knew he would get the whole story if he waited patiently. Chip always thought things out pretty thoroughly before he talked about them to anyone.

Out front, behind the soda fountain counter, an impatient Petey Jackson focused his sharp eyes on the storeroom door. He was anxious to surprise Chip with his Baseball Quiz. Petey had been working on the questions for a week and hadn't shown them to a single soul; he couldn't stand it any longer. His watchfulness was rewarded when he saw the door open.

"Hey, Chip, come here! I got something to show you. C'mon!"

A moment later, a reluctant Chip was gazing at a piece of paper, which the freckle-faced manager held proudly in his skinny hand.

"Look at these questions! Betcha don't know a third of 'em!"

"No-o-o!" groaned Chip. "Don't tell me you're up to that again!" He gripped his head and assumed a pained expression. "Please, Petey, anything but that!" He pushed Petey back behind the fountain. "You promised to quit," he said accusingly.

For a moment Petey was discouraged. But only for a moment. "Hey, look who's here!" He pointed to a dejected Soapy Smith entering the front door.

"Hey, Soapy, c'mere." Petey waved the paper in the air. "I've got a surprise for ya."

But Soapy wasn't interested. He joined Chip, and they sat down at one of the corner tables. Petey gave up in disgust.

LIKE FATHER—LIKE SON

Chip explained to Soapy that Rockwell was really bawling out the whole squad that afternoon. The same thing had happened to him last year. "Don't worry about it. He'll be all right tomorrow," Chip reassured his friend.

"But what if he won't give me another chance?" Soapy moaned. "I gotta make that team this year!"

"He'll give you another chance! You have to break training rules, get in trouble at school, or do something clear out of line before the Rock'll really drop you."

A little later, a much-relieved Soapy Smith left the Sugar Bowl. He didn't even pause for a hamburger and fries or a hot fudge sundae. Petey Jackson looked after Soapy in amazement. "What d'ya know!" he exclaimed. "What d'ya know! This might be a first."

At eight o'clock, Chip heard the ponderous footsteps of Doc Jones in his office above the Sugar Bowl. The old doctor was about the only man in Valley Falls heavy enough to make the ceiling shake.

When Chip knocked and entered, Doc Jones was sitting in a comfortable chair, gloomily surveying the littered contents of the pigeonholes in his desk. Every one was crammed full of letters and papers. Bills, prescription pads, and old newspapers were scattered carelessly on the flat surface of the desk; some letters had never been opened.

Doc Jones gestured toward the desk. "Someday I'm going to clean that thing up, Chip. Maybe I ought to wait until winter to do it though. Weather's too nice now. I'd hire a cleaning service, but they won't take the job," he chuckled. He turned quickly and peered over his glasses at Chip. "What's on your mind?"

Chip wasted no time. "I thought you said my leg was all right."

"It is!"

"Well, then, what's the matter with the coach? He won't let me run."

"Now look here, William Hilton," Jones began. "I told you that leg was all right, and it is! Remember when I cut the front out of the cast so you could exercise your leg? Well, you exercised it a lot before I gave you the brace, but the muscles need to be stronger. They've come along a little slower.

"I want you to exercise that ankle at every opportunity—even in bed! Keep stretching it! I can create some kind of spring and hook it to the foot of your bed, and then while you're going to sleep, keep stretching the ankle.

"Don't worry! Before the first game rolls around, you'll be sitting pretty!"

"Sure!" Chip said dejectedly. "Sitting's right! Sitting right on the bench! I had enough of that during the basketball season. I've got competition for my spot! *Real* competition!"

CHAPTER 3

Now or Never

THE *YELLOW JACKET,* the Valley Falls High School paper, was published weekly and put on sale each Friday at noon in the foyer of the gym. Chip purchased his copy and leaned against one of the trophy cases. He always enjoyed the paper because it was written and edited by the students. Even several basketball articles he had written during the past hoops season had appeared in the paper. He turned to the sports section and was attracted to a column right smack in the middle of the page.

THE BATTING CAGE

IS sentiment playing a part in the persistence of Coach Rockwell's keeping Chip Hilton behind the plate when it is obvious that Hilton isn't going to be able to do heavy work because of his injured ankle? Wouldn't Chip be more valuable to the team as a pinch hitter than as a handicapped receiver?

STRIKE THREE!

ISN'T it true that most baseball coaches want the fielder with the best arm in right field? Is Coach Rockwell keeping Mike Rodriguez in that position because he was a star basketball player?

IS there any truth in the rumor that Nick Trullo, who shapes up as the best pitching prospect for this year's team, stated he would pitch to Carl Carey or to no one?

Chip read the article twice before walking across the hall to the trophy case. He gazed down at the new shiny basketball won by Valley Falls in the state championship game at the end of the past season. Across the front in white letters was stenciled WILLIAM "CHIP" HILTON. Directly next to that ball was another and across the front of that one, too, was printed WILLIAM "CHIP" HILTON. The latter ball was faded and old but was far more precious to Chip than the new one.

A long-standing tradition at Valley Falls honored the player who had contributed most to the winning of any championship with the stenciling of his or her name on the game ball. Then the ball was shellacked and placed in the appropriate trophy case for everyone to see.

Chip's thoughts went back over the past basketball season. Because of his injured ankle, he had been unable to play but had been the team manager. His teammates had awarded him the ball right after the championship game with Rutledge.

Big Chip Hilton had won the honor because of his leadership and play on the court. *Humph, some comparison,* Chip reflected bitterly. Well, there wasn't going to be any more of that. He'd win whatever honors came his way from now on by playing! Doc Jones said his leg was all right. Carey, Trullo, and the rest of them would see *now* whether Chip Hilton was through!

He opened the paper again and studied the baseball schedule. Eight games at home, five away, and then the state championship games at the university. "If we only had good pitching," he murmured, "we might do it!"

BASEBALL SCHEDULE

Sat.	April 23	WESTON		Home
Fri.	April 29	PARKTON		Home
Sat.	May 7	SOUTHERN		Away
Fri.	May 13	SEABURG	Sec. IV	Home
Sat.	May 21	DULANE		Home
Wed.	May 25	SALEM		Away
Sat.	May 28	DELFORD		Home
Wed.	June 1	COREYVILLE	Sec. I	Away
Sat.	June 4	STRATFORD		Away
Wed.	June 8	DANE		Home
Sat.	June 11	DELFORD		Away
Wed.	June 15	EDGEMONT	Sec. III	Home
Sat.	June 18	STEELTOWN		Home

The Sectional Champions will meet at the university on Friday, June 24, and on Saturday, June 25, to decide the State High School (Class A) Championship.

Rockwell was talking to the squad in the bleachers when Chip reached the field. As he trotted up, everyone started for the sliding pit. Pop Brown, Valley Falls trainer, had just finished smoothing the sawdust.

Chet Stewart came flying into the pit at full speed to demonstrate the correct slides. Then Rockwell asked him to come in slow-motion. This was a difficult maneuver but one of Rockwell's favorite coaching procedures. An outsider who knew little about sports—about baseball—would have laughed to see Stewart taking slow, almost tiptoe, steps as if he were trying to slip up behind someone. But there wasn't anything funny about it to the eager boys who watched so intently. Rockwell believed in speed and in baserunning, and in Rockwell's coaching, everything started with form.

Rockwell explained each step in the various slides, halting and holding Stewart in each position and part of the maneuver he wanted to discuss or stress. Stewart had completed the hook slide and was lying with his left toe hooked into the canvas base while he rested on his right hip. His right leg was outstretched, and his arms were held loose over his head.

"Note that Chet tilts his spikes *up* when he hits the pit. Why is that, Morris?"

The barrel-chested shortstop nudged Chip and stepped forward. "So he won't catch 'em in the ground and turn or break an ankle," he explained.

As far as size and build were concerned, Speed Morris might have been another Rockwell. He had the same stocky build, the same black hair and eyes, and the same quick gestures. He was aptly named. Only Chip, Speed's best friend, could outrun him in the hundred. But Chip couldn't match Speed on the base paths. Chip's long legs needed time to lengthen out. Speed's shorter, powerful legs got him into high gear instantly—that was important in the ninety-foot dash between bases.

"That's right! And that's why we use the pit for practice. We'll keep away from sliding on the field until we master form. Remember, the ground's soft now, but in another six or eight weeks, it'll be hard. And then, if you ride into a base with careless, untrained spikes, they may catch in the hard ground and ruin an ankle. Let's get form first, speed later!"

One by one the boys took their turns, coming into the pit in slow-motion. Chip lined up for his turn, but Rockwell stopped him.

"Never mind, Chip. You watch!"

Chip swallowed hard. It was now or never.

"I'd like to take my turn, Coach. Doc Jones told me last night my leg is all right. Watch, Coach!"

He turned, dashed down the path at full speed, and threw himself into the sawdust. It was a beautiful bent-leg slide, and at the end Chip thrust his injured left ankle viciously into the bag Pop placed in the center of the pit after each slide. Months of pent-up sports desire went into that flying spurt. Chip wouldn't have deviated from the wild abandon of that charge and slide if he had been dashing into a pile of rocks. He was trying to prove something to the coach, but he was trying to prove more to himself.

Rockwell's eyes flashed to Chet Stewart, and a look of understanding passed between them.

"Nice slide, Chip," he said. "Ankle must be all right if you can take off like that!" He turned to the silent players who had been watching the sliding action. "All right, we'll all come in on the run now. But be careful!"

After each player took his turn, Rockwell ordered the boys back to the bleachers. While they were getting settled, he stood in front of the stands, hefting a bat in his hands. When they quieted, he began.

"Batting is an individual skill, just like shooting a basketball. Some players have natural ability, some don't. Some acquire it, some don't! Almost every hitter can benefit by proper practice, but there are certain athletes who don't want to pay a price for anything. They want to drift in with the breeze.

"Maybe Chet Stewart and Bill Thomas and I can't teach you to hit, but we can try. We've been in this baseball game a long time. We have three rules to hit by: get a good pitch to hit, think properly, and be quick with the bat.

"Be aggressive with the bat. Focus on your strike zone and make the pitcher put the ball in the zone. It's a skill to hit the ball, so there's no sense trying to swing at balls outside the zone.

"Next, know the pitcher. What's his best pitch? What did he throw you last time? What does he throw on the first pitch? Know what's going on before you step into the batter's box. Think.

"Last, when you decide to swing, give it your very best swing—not a wimpy, halfhearted attempt. That small distinction may make the difference between an easy out and a solid line drive.

"Now, we want to study your stance and your swing. Remember the wrists have a lot to do with hitting—especially for the slow stuff. We want to study you at the plate, but we don't want to study kids who try to hit every ball out of the park.

"Keep your eye on the ball and just try to meet it! Get your timing for a week or so, then we'll open up and give you some real pitching and get a line on your hitting under pressure."

Rockwell turned to Pop Brown. "Pop, bring the board over here, will you? We'll do a little schoolwork now!"

Chip sat in the bleachers thinking about Rockwell's coaching methods. Not many coaches would have a board out on the baseball field the first week in April. The Rock was a great believer in having his players—in any sport—think through his reasons for a particular training technique or sports principle.

"The swing's the thing!" Rockwell quipped. "Now let's look at why we like our hitters to be in a stand-up position at the plate. There's only one real reason. So the hitter has only to lower his body to meet any kind of pitch.

"The player who crouches at the plate has to raise and lower his body for the different pitches. We eliminate the raising by teaching a stand-up position."

Rockwell assumed a relaxed stance with his feet in a comfortable position about six to eight inches wider than his shoulders. "Now," he said, "I can hit a ball across the letters, or by dipping my knees a bit, I can level off on a low pitch.

"Level off is something you'll hear as long as you play baseball. In the big leagues or in high school—wherever baseball players meet—the term is understood. I'll use the board to make it clear to you." He turned and drew several diagrams.

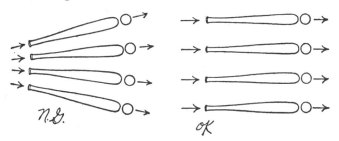

"I'm not much of an artist," Rockwell chuckled, "but I'm sure everyone here can tell which represents a level bat and which represents a reaching or dropping bat. A player can level off on a pitch across the letters by standing upright, and then for the lower pitches, all he has to do is drop his body a bit. And that brings us to something else."

Rockwell searched through the squad until his eyes settled on Chip. "Hilton, what is that something else that is just as important as hitting with a level bat?"

Chip scratched the back of his head reflectively, squinting into the afternoon sun. "Guess it's keeping the shoulders level, too, Coach," he said, watching Rockwell closely.

"Why level the shoulders?"

"Because that keeps you from chopping down or cutting under the ball. When you drop your front shoulder, you sort of chop at the ball, and when you drop your rear shoulder, you cut under the ball and lift it in the air."

Rockwell flashed Chip a quick smile. "Right!" he said. "That's why Hilton is a good hitter, boys. He keeps his shoulders and his bat level. And . . . he keeps a level head too." His black eyes focused intently on Chip's gray, alert eyes and held there for a brief second. Then he added, "Usually!" before turning to Biggie Cohen and handing him the bat.

"Biggie, show us how you stand in the batter's box."

Cohen's big hands almost swallowed the bat. The power seemed to flow visibly down his strong forearms as he assumed his batting stance and gently moved the bat forward and back.

"Now, boys," Rockwell continued, "Biggie is a power hitter. He gets a lot of wrist action in his swing. Watch! Go ahead, Biggie."

Cohen stilled the movement of the bat, concentrated on an imaginary pitcher, then moved his bat slightly backward and started his swing. As the bat came forward, Biggie took a short forward step and snapped the bat forward at full speed with a flip of his wrists.

Rockwell analyzed each part of Cohen's swing. He brought out that Biggie's preliminary waggles of the bat came only after he had taken his position in the batter's box. The little waggles were taken to loosen up the wrists and forearms. When the pitcher started his windup, the bat was held motionless. Then, as the ball was released, Biggie cocked his wrists by the tiny backward motion and leveled off with shoulders and bat, trying to meet the ball slightly in front of the plate.

"Note that Biggie almost explodes the bat into the ball. He rolls his wrists through with the bat. His arms are loose, too, and form a *V* away from his body.

"Now, a moment ago, I spoke about an open stance. Clean that board off, Pop. I think I can show you what I mean."

Rockwell drew several figures on the board.

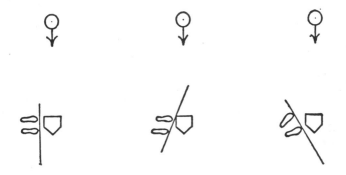

"The diagram of the feet on the left shows a straight stance. Note the feet are pointed directly at the plate.

"The diagram in the middle represents the feet of a batter with a closed stance. The left foot is closer to the plate than the right.

"The last diagram illustrates the position of the feet in an open stance.

"When a player uses a straight or a closed stance, his shoulders are square with the plate, and his head is turned in an unnatural position so he can watch the ball. With an open stance, the batter's shoulders are diagonal to the plate, and his head is in a more natural position. He can follow the ball more easily and is generally in more of a ready position. We'll use an open stance for a week or so, concentrating on stride, swing, and follow-through.

"Chet, you and Bill take the players over there behind the batting cage and work on their stance and hitting positions. Make 'em all choke up a bit. Let me have a man on deck and one in the hole for every batter so I can keep the hitters moving. Chip, you warm up Trullo; Carey, you take Peters. I'll lob a few to the hitters until the pitchers are ready.

"You pitchers—no curves and no fancy stuff! Just give the batter a straight pitch. I'm not interested in fast stuff. Work on your control! Remember, we're working on batting! Furthermore, I prefer pitchers who have sense enough to take care of their arms. I like pitchers with good heads and strong arms, and I've no use at all for pitchers with big heads and sore arms!"

When Chip's turn came to bat, he felt confident. The practice swings he had been taking every day through the football and basketball seasons had given him the feel of a bat. He met three of Rockwell's pitches freely and easily, and the ball took off each time on a line.

The Thursday practice concentrated on the hit-and-run play. Rockwell explained that the important things in the hit-and-run are to make contact with the ball and to hit behind the runner.

"However," he said, "there are exceptions. For example, when a lefty is up, most second basemen will stay in position and let the shortstop cover second base. Here, place hitting is important. We'll concentrate on making contact and getting the ball on the ground.

"Big-league hitters try to hit through the hole left by the infielder covering the bag. The runner on first can help the batter find out whether the second baseman or the shortstop is going to cover by taking a trial run and watching the reaction of the infielders."

Rockwell paused and smiled at the eager faces. "But that'll have to wait. The pros can't have any of you fellows until you're at least through high school. Get that diploma."

Soapy Smith took off his cap and struck it across his knees. A pained expression covered his face. "Just my luck!" he cried. He heaved a dramatic sigh and then continued in a resigned voice, "They'll just have to wait, that's all!"

CHAPTER 4

Play with His Mind

SOAPY SMITH tapped the handle of his favorite bat on the ground and surveyed the cracked surface ruefully. "What we need around here is a bat boy!" he growled.

"You'll do just fine!" Red Schwartz declared.

"Aw, I wouldn't want to beat you out of the job," Soapy retorted. "Besides, what makes you think you've got this team made?"

Chip, swinging three bats, waited for his turn to bat. He reviewed the past week's progress. After the sliding-pit incident, Rockwell had made no attempt to stop his play. So far his ankle was all right. He had worked hard, giving his leg no lenience, and he was just as unyielding in his relationships with Trullo and Carey.

Carey was a good receiver. His footwork was good, and although his arm was not as strong as Chip's, he shaped up well. When it came to hitting, however, Carl wasn't in Chip's class. Chip had led all Valley Falls hitters the previous year, batting over the .500 mark. Rockwell had alternated Chip between the cleanup spot and the fifth position in the batting order for the past two years.

Unaccountably, Chip's thoughts swung to Tim Murphy. Chip had succeeded to Murphy's position as star passer of the football team. At least, Pete Williams of the *Post* and Joe Kennedy of the *Times* had said so. Wouldn't it be something if he could become a pitcher like Tim? Then Carey could have the catching job, but not unless Chip Hilton got a chance to pitch!

The surprise of the early practice sessions had been the playing of Chris Badger at third base and the double-play combination of veteran Speed Morris and the new-comer, Cody Collins. All week, the Rock had spent a short period of each practice around the keystone sack.

Cody proved to be a great prospect at second. He had a strong arm, and his natural aggressiveness marked him as the infield pepperbox that Rockwell always liked to have chattering away and spicing up his teams.

Rockwell had timed Speed and Cody on the double play. He claimed a successful double play in the major leagues had to be performed in less than 4½ seconds. That is, from the time the ball left the pitcher's hand until it hit the first baseman's glove, by way of the second baseman and the shortstop, the time consumed must not exceed that limit.

"Of course," he admitted wryly, "if you boys can do it in five seconds most of the time, I'll be satisfied."

Chip guessed he would, too, since the new combination hadn't been clocked at much better than seven seconds so far. But Chip knew the Rock. The Rock was a stickler for details. He'd be on Speed and Cody—eliminating a little wasted motion here, a step there—until they got their time down to where they could make their share of that most important defensive play.

STRIKE THREE!

Soapy came back from his turn at bat, and Chip was up. He hit the very first pitch with perfect timing, and the ball sailed over the right-field fence. Valley Falls Field was built to order for Chip. Its right-field fence was short and a good target for Chip's left-hand shots. Chip was naturally right-handed, but his father had started him swinging from the portside when he was a little kid. Chip favored the left-handed batting position, but he was a switch hitter; he could bat well from the other side of the plate and often did against southpaw pitchers.

A shrill blast from Rockwell's whistle assembled the squad in front of the batting cage. Rockwell held a bat lightly in his hands.

"We'll work a bit on bunting," he began. "Many a good pitcher has been bunted clear out of the ballpark because he never learned to field his position. Lots of times a bunt may be necessary to put the winning run in position for a score, and sometimes we may be able to squeeze an important run across the plate with a clever bunt."

Rockwell coached each player in turn, stressing the importance of body position and keeping the bat level. The boys were told to hold the bat out in front and to keep their arms away from the body. He explained that a good bunter keeps his bat level just as in hitting and uses it as a cushion. He warned against stroking the ball or trying to cut down, up, or back. He emphasized that dragging or pushing a bunt was a matter of practice.

"When you become more proficient in meeting the ball, or rather letting the ball meet the bat, we'll try to teach you how to conceal the bunt as long as possible. OK?"

After the bunting practice, Rockwell called for a three-inning practice game. "We'll play it just like a regular game," he announced. "Chet, you take team B over there to the visiting team dugout, and I'll stay on this side with team A. Bill, you umpire!"

Team A lined up with Chip behind the plate, Nick Trullo pitching, Biggie Cohen on first base, Cody Collins on second, Speed Morris at shortstop, Chris Badger at third base, Ted Williams in left field, Red Schwartz in center field, and Mike Rodriguez in right field. Lefty Peters and Carl Carey made up the battery for team B.

Bill Thomas grabbed an old mask and dashed to the plate. "All right," he called, "let's go!"

Team A took the field, and Chip walked to the mound. "You want the usual signs, Nick?" he asked.

Trullo barely glanced at him. "Yeah, sure. Whatever!" he said sullenly, shrugging his shoulders.

"Play ball!" Bill Thomas crouched behind Chip, and the practice game was on.

Chip called for a fastball, and Trullo powered the first pitch through the heart of the plate, but that was the last time Chip's signs and Trullo's pitches matched. When the inning was over, Chip waited for Trullo on the way to the dugout.

"What's the use of me giving you the signs, Nick?" Chip challenged. "You don't pitch what I call for."

"Well, don't give any then!" Trullo growled fiercely.

Chip's gray eyes narrowed and his thin lips tightened in a straight line, but he said nothing more. If that was the way Trullo wanted it, that was the way it would be.

Fortunately, team B was made up of weak reserves, and Trullo had a field day. He held them to one scratch hit in the three-inning game. Little Lefty Peters didn't fare so well. The varsity players knew him well because of his pitching for batting practice. They teed off and hit almost everything he threw. In fact, Lefty wasn't able to get team A out in the last of the third, and Rockwell called the game.

STRIKE THREE!

Carl Carey had caught a nice game, but he was slowly earning the dislike of player after player on the B squad. As a catcher, he was a little slow in getting the ball away, and Red Schwartz and Speed had gone down to second on clean steals. What antagonized the players, however, was Carey's sarcastic needling, which had a little too much edge in it to be meant purely in fun. During the practice game he had worked on Biggie Cohen. Biggie was a quiet, easygoing guy until he was stepped on. Then, watch out!

"Pin the big bozo's ears back, Lefty," Carey had called.

Just as Biggie had started his movement to swing, Carl tipped Cohen's bat with his glove. The ball had sped across the plate for a called strike. Biggie had stepped back from the plate and eyed Carey carefully and silently.

After practice, Chip, Speed, and Biggie hurried through their showers and piled into Speed's car. Chip felt better than he had for a long time. Although Nick Trullo had deliberately disregarded his signs, Chip passed the matter over lightly and resolved to wait until the first game. Maybe Nick would get over it.

The talk swung around to Trullo and Carey.

"Everyone's gettin' to hate those two guys!" Speed remarked thoughtfully. "What's eatin' them anyway?"

"Gettin' hung up on themselves, I guess," Cohen said shortly. "Personally, I don't like that stuff Carey's pullin' behind the plate. He'd better be careful! The next time he starts razzin' me and bumps my bat with his glove, I'm going to pick him up and give that little boy a spankin'."

The minute Chip entered the Sugar Bowl that night, he realized something was troubling Petey Jackson. Chip knew the skinny little fountain manager like a brother.

Petey hurried from behind the fountain. "Say, Chip! You know Sorelli's place."

PLAY WITH HIS MIND

Chip knew Petey Jackson was about the best straight pool player in town. Petey's long, slender fingers were nimble and strong, and he had a good eye.

"Well, I was in there the other night after we closed up, and, Chip—" Petey glanced surreptitiously around and lowered his voice—"I overheard something I think you ought to know! I've been worryin' about it ever since!"

"What?"

"You know Carl Carey's brother? Well, he was talking to a couple of those older South Side guys, and I heard one of them say, 'Work on Nick then!' And then Ken Carey says, 'Nick wouldn't do anything like that.' And then this other guy says, 'Play it smart! Use psychology! Play with his mind. Nick hates Hilton, doesn't he?' And then Ken answers, 'So what?' Then this other guy yells, 'So what? Nick's the only pitcher on the team, isn't he? And Hilton's the regular catcher, isn't he?'"

Petey looked at Chip anxiously.

"Then they must have seen me looking at them because they moved back into a corner."

Petey paused to check out the story's effect on Chip. "Now, what do you think that was all about?"

Chip shook his head uncertainly. "You've got me, Petey," he said slowly. "I don't know. Who were the two men talking to Ken?"

"Aw, you know, those two who are always causin' trouble down at the poolroom—that Peck Weaver and Buck Adams."

Chip knew both Weaver and Adams by sight and by reputation. He didn't want to know them any better. He did know Ken Carey, who had always seemed like a good guy.

"Maybe you misunderstood them, Petey—"

STRIKE THREE!

But Petey was persistent. "No, I didn't, Chip. I distinctly heard them say just what I've told you, and they used your name. Not once, but lotsa times!"

Chip shrugged his shoulders. "Couldn't have been very important, Petey. Forget it!"

But Chip couldn't and didn't forget it.

CHAPTER 5

"Sunday Pitch"

TAPS BROWNING craned his long neck over Soapy Smith's shoulder as the ball came flying toward home plate in the Hilton A. C. The ball slapped into Big Chip Hilton's old glove with a crack that resounded throughout the neighborhood like a slammed door. Soapy had the knack of doing that with a fast one; he could pinch a ball into his glove and smother the impact, or he could open the big mitt wide and allow the flying sphere to strike the hard-packed surface at full speed.

Chip followed his throw with one step and crouched in front of the little mound with his hands in position near his knees, ready to field an imaginary hit. Biggie Cohen stood behind Chip, showing him how a pitcher fielded his position.

"Wow!" yelled Soapy. "Did that one smoke or did it smoke?"

Taps Browning exhaled a deep breath. "Man, it's a good thing Soapy caught that one," he said. "I couldn't have dodged that pitch to save my life!"

STRIKE THREE!

Speed Morris regarded Soapy curiously. "Ya know," he said, "you almost look like a catcher!"

Soapy lifted an eyebrow and sighed patiently. "Look like a catcher? I've got history, man. I was a battery mate for one of Valley Falls's immortals—the one and only Tim Murphy. I grew up playing catch with Tim. I used to catch him in his backyard, just like we're doing here today with Chip!"

Soapy scratched his red hair and glanced hesitantly at Chip. "If . . . if Rock hadn't used Chip as catcher last year, I was gonna ask—"

"Why didn't you?" demanded Chip. "Soapy, Rock was looking for another catcher all last year."

"That's right," agreed Speed. "Chip had to catch every game!" He was struck with an idea. "Hey! You know something?" He shook a closed fist around the little circle. "Let's get Chip ready to pitch and Soapy to catch. Then, if the Rock ever needs a battery, he'll have one all set. You guys can work up your signs for waste pitches, pitchouts, and pickoffs. Then you'll be ready to step right into the box anytime. How about it?"

"We'll kill 'em," shouted Soapy, dancing around in a circle and holding the big catcher's glove on top of his head. "We'll kill 'em!"

Chip grinned ruefully. "It sure sounds simple," he said, "but there's a lot of difference between throwing a ball in the backyard and in a regular game. And how do I know I can even pitch?"

"*I* know you can pitch," Soapy stated emphatically. "Guess I ought to know. I played catch with Murphy for years back of his house. You're faster! You throw a harder ball, Chip!"

Speed nodded his head. "Yeah, and Tim Murphy didn't do so bad with a fastball, man!"

"We can do it," affirmed Soapy.

"We?" echoed Speed. "Who's we?"

Soapy pretended superiority. "It breaks my heart to blow my own horn. Ahem. S'pose we just say, we'll work it out together!"

Sitting on the Hilton back porch, Suzy Browning and Little Paddy Jackson watched the boys. Suzy poorly pretended she had no interest in Soapy Smith while Paddy exhibited extreme boredom. Now, he had to have a little action. He leaped from his faithful baby-sitter's side and abruptly demanded, "I want a ball!"

Speed turned and mimicked the redheaded, freckle-faced miniature edition of the Sugar Bowl's fountain manager. "So you want a ball!" He stopped suddenly and pointed a finger at the little boy. "Paddy Jackson—that's it!" he yelled.

"You're absolutely right!" Soapy agreed. Then he stopped. "What's it?" he asked curiously.

"We need a bat boy, don't we?" Speed began patiently.

In a few minutes, they all agreed that Paddy Jackson was just what the Big Reds needed to make their season a success. The next half hour was spent in hilarious instruction of Paddy in the art of being a bat boy.

While Biggie showed the little boy how to arrange the bats and tried to impress him with the importance of keeping every bat in its proper place, Chip absentmindedly threw the ball against the back fence, fielding it after the rebound as it rolled along the ground.

"Hey!" Speed yelled again. "I've got *another* brilliant idea! Why don't we fix up some boards there on the back fence and mark out the strike zone above an imaginary plate so Chip can practice. He won't even need a catcher. That way, when he's home alone, he can practice by himself."

STRIKE THREE!

"You've got something there, Speed," Biggie said enthusiastically. "Let's fix it right now!"

Taps Browning hopped the fence and soon returned with a saw, several hammers, and a jar full of nails. In the next hour, the amateur carpenters constructed an imaginary batter and a strike zone on the back fence. Soapy and Speed made a quick trip in the car to the hardware store and came back with brushes and red and white paint. Then, a comical Soapy Smith skillfully painted the outline of a man on the fence and lettered in the name "ROCK" where the baseball cap should have been. "Now," he muttered, "now, you can try your fastball on that hard head!"

After they measured off the sixty feet, six inches from the pitching rubber to the point where the first- and third-base lines met at home plate directly under the fence, Chip had an automatic catcher. They breathed in satisfaction as they admired their work.

"Throw a few, Chip. Try it out," Biggie urged.

Chip threw the ball against the reinforced strike zone, and the ball came bounding back almost as though it had been hit by a batter.

"I can throw fast enough," Chip said slowly, "but I don't know about my control. And I've got to have a curveball or something for a change-of-pace pitch."

Speed Morris grunted. "Listen," he said. "Anyone who can toss a football like you isn't going to have any trouble with a little thing like a baseball. Just look at that hand! All you need to do, my friend, is to throw every day and get the feel of it. Control, hah! You'll have control!"

"Chip's right though, Speed," said Biggie. "A pitcher's got to have a curve: a little one, a medium one, and a big one. Chip's got a lot of speed, and control's a matter of practice. But a change-of-pace ball—he's gotta have it!"

"SUNDAY PITCH"

"Well, get it!" said Speed. "You don't have to be born with a curve, do you?"

"It might help," Biggie said, laughing, "but pitching's a matter of practice and sorta specializing on some particular pitch—"

Soapy saw an opening. "You mean a 'Sunday pitch,'" he said, beaming.

Speed swung the bat over his head and playfully chased Soapy up on the back porch. "Sunday pitch!" he mimicked. "You and your wisecracks!"

"That really isn't so funny," said Biggie. "After all, every pitcher has a specialty that's known as his Sunday pitch. Chip throws a heavy ball every time he throws sidearm. That could be his specialty. A sidearm pitch with a sinker or something he does to make the ball move."

Soapy shoved his way into the center of the circle. "What about me?" he asked belligerently. "What do I practice?"

Soapy asked for it and he got it!

"A catcher must have a lot of pep; he has to be tough."

Biggie's lecture continued. "The catcher is in reality the quarterback of the team when they are in the field. He crouches close to the batter, gives the signals to the pitcher and the basemen, always takes the same position and holds his hands the same way for every pitch, always gives the pitcher a good target, keeps his body in front of the pitch by shifting his feet, has to have a strong arm, and knows how to throw to all bases.

"The catcher has to call the plays for the mound when the pitcher is fielding a ball, has to be able to field the bunts in front of the plate and master quick throwing to the proper base, has to know how to block runners at home and how to tag them holding the ball firmly in the glove—"

STRIKE THREE!

Chip interrupted Biggie. "Don't ever risk tagging a runner with the ball in the bare hand, Soapy, unless the throw draws you out of position. It's too easy for the runner to knock the ball out of your hand."

Soapy's head was buzzing. Fortunately for him, the discussion was interrupted by the sound of Mrs. Hilton's engine as she pulled her car into the garage. Paddy scrambled his skinny, paint-streaked legs toward the garage, wanting to be the first to help Chip's mom unload groceries. Soapy was hard on his heels, laughing and chasing after the squealing little boy.

After glancing quickly through its contents, Soapy magnanimously volunteered to carry one large bag to the house. Chip and Speed couldn't resist a shared chuckle as they noticed the large bag of potato chips proudly protruding from the grocery bag like the sail of a schooner ship.

A little later, Taps handed Paddy over the fence to Suzy, and Speed, Biggie, and Soapy started home. "Well," began Biggie, as they stopped a moment at the gate before leaving Chip, "I think we did a good job this afternoon."

"Me too!" agreed Speed. "Now the first time the Rock needs a battery, he'll have one!"

"He'll have a *dazzling* one!" corrected Soapy. "But how will he know it?"

"He'll know it!" Biggie said firmly. "You just get ready, Chip. And Soapy too. That's the important thing—to be prepared when the opportunity comes."

CHAPTER 6

South Side, West Side

THE SOUTH SIDE of Valley Falls was built on a hill that ran almost down to the edge of Valley River. The houses, perched precariously against the hill's abrupt rise, were small, single-family homes with small lawns. Most were in good shape, but some properties showed signs of neglect.

The West Side, directly across the river, was built on a hill leading up from the river too. But on this side of the river, the hill ascended gracefully in a series of little terraces that were ideal for the construction of larger, more expensive homes.

The business section of Valley Falls was located close to the river on the West Side, but the sloping hill was devoted exclusively to residences. The majority of the West Side inhabitants were professionals or people who held white-collar positions, while the South Side residents were primarily blue-collar workers. Many of them were employed by the pottery or the lumberyard. There was also a small group of the frequently unemployed.

The South Side boys sprang from generations of rugged stock; they played hard and intensely. Coach Rockwell was always glad to see them out for his teams. Although the situation was improving with time, some of the South Side families were not financially able to send their boys all the way through high school, and occasionally one of the most promising athletes dropped out of school to go to work. Thus, the pendulum moving between West Side and South Side athletic representation on the high school teams seldom swung far in either direction. For the past two years, the West-Siders had been in the majority.

It was customary for those South Side athletes who dropped out of high school to play seasonal sports on the independent and industrial teams of Valley Falls. Additionally, every Sunday, the South Side residents, young and old, would gather on the "Hill" to watch or play whatever sport was currently in season. The Hill was a large level area that topped the South Side.

This Sunday, baseball was the game, and the Hill was crowded. Ken Carey, Carl Carey's older brother, was seated on a large rock watching the action on the field. The two men with him were Peck Weaver and Buck Adams. Weaver was talking to Carey.

"Here come Nick and Carl now. Go to work on 'em!"

Ken Carey gestured impatiently. "I've *been* working on them, Peck. Why can't you guys come up with some other way? Have a heart—they're both good kids!"

"Sure they are! So what? They don't have to do nothin' wrong."

"But—"

Weaver pushed him roughly and spat on the ground menacingly. "No buts! You play ball with us, or the whole

SOUTH SIDE, WEST SIDE

South Side's gonna know about Leroy White! And your brother will be the first one to be told. Count on it!"

"Yeah, and my old man happens to be your boss at the pottery," drawled Adams with a sneer playing around his lips. "Get it?"

Ken Carey sighed. "OK," he breathed, "OK!"

Nick Trullo and Carl Carey worked as battery mates in the game that followed. They clearly demonstrated that the coaching they were receiving from Rockwell and his staff was beneficial. Both showed poise in their positions, and their battery efforts were successful. Trullo was too fast and a little too wild for the batters. He had the upper hand though, and he kept them at his mercy all afternoon.

Ken Carey watched his brother proudly, and after the game ended, he and the two men with him walked home with the boys. Ken Carey had to support his mom, brother, and sister, and only Ken's insistence had kept Carl in high school the times he'd talked about quitting. Ken was determined to see his little brother through community college and maybe even watch him go on to University someday.

Carl had always admired Ken for being so good to their mother and the family, but his greatest pride had been in his older brother's standing with the Hill crowd. Ken was constantly in the company of Peck Weaver and Buck Adams, and that stamped him as a person to be respected. Weaver and Adams were recognized as two of the most intimidating young men on the South Side, and no one wanted to cross them or any of their friends.

"You're getting so you can blaze 'em right past the hitters up here on the Hill, Nick," Ken said admiringly.

"You ought to have the number-one pitching assignment all wrapped up over there at the high school," Weaver added.

"He's the man," agreed Adams.

Nick flushed. He wasn't used to compliments from these guys. He was pleased, and he wanted to please these men in return. He glanced at Carl.

"Carl helps me a lot—"

"What about Carl?" Adams broke in quickly. "He gonna make the team?"

Nick's eyes flashed angrily. "He would if it wasn't for Rockwell's pet—the great Hilton!"

"*You* don't like him, I can see that," Weaver said.

Adams laughed. "And from what I hear, he hasn't any use for you either, Nick." He elbowed Ken Carey. "That right, Ken?"

Ken nodded. "Umm, that's right, I guess," he said.

The three men paused on a corner, and the two boys continued home alone. There was a pleased expression on the faces of Weaver and Adams, but Ken Carey's eyes were troubled.

After the Sunday evening rush had passed at the Sugar Bowl, Chip headed for the storeroom. Sitting in John Schroeder's desk chair, he began to think about pitching. In his mind he set up imaginary situations on the baseball diamond. He was the pitcher in each case, and he tried to figure out his correct response.

There was a man on first and none down. How did he wind up? Wind up? In that situation, a good pitcher didn't wind up but pitched from the set position. He held the ball in the stretch, between high-stretched arms over his head, and pitched without a windup. He could lower his arms and hold glove and pitching hands together in front of the body if he wished, but he couldn't remove either from the ball or make any motion toward a base or home plate without throwing the ball, or he'd commit a balk.

A good pitcher kept watching the runners. He threw a couple or three to first when a base runner was fast. With a man on third—depending upon the situation—he watched him carefully so that the runner didn't get too big a lead. There was always the possibility of an attempt to steal home. A right-handed pitcher could keep runners on third worried easily, just like a lefty could worry a runner on first.

At home and in bed, Chip manipulated Doc's hand-crafted ankle exerciser and let his thoughts review the past week. What was in the Rock's mind about solving the pitching problem? How could he bring his own pitching dreams to Rockwell's attention? He was sure of one thing: he was going to throw every day and develop control. If correct repetition was the secret of success, he'd keep striking out the batter on the back fence until he got it right—or until he wore a hole in the fence.

His thoughts flew to the sports festival that would be held at the University next Friday and Saturday. Maybe he'd get to go again. Well, if he didn't, someday maybe he'd be at State and be an All-American as his father had been.

It was a slow week for Chip. He was anxious to know who would get the call for the sports festival. He and everyone else found out on Thursday. A release was sent out from the university naming the fortunate athletes from all over the state who had been invited to attend the festival as guests of the State Athletic Department. First on the Valley Falls list was the name of Chip Hilton. Then followed Speed Morris, Biggie Cohen, and Taps Browning.

At nine o'clock Friday morning, Chip waited at the Sugar Bowl for the arrival of his friends and Coach Rockwell. The selection of Speed and Biggie had been no surprise to Chip, but Taps Browning was a puzzle. He had always thought a player had to be at least a two-letter man, and Taps had played only basketball for a single year. As he waited, Chip thought ruefully, "Guess that means I must be riding on last year's reputation."

The drive to University was a three-hour trip. Coach Rockwell drove his car, and Biggie was seated beside him. Chip, Speed, and Taps were in the back seat. Just before they had pulled away from the Sugar Bowl, Petey Jackson had come rushing out with food.

"Just in case you don't have time to stop or go to a drive-through. Besides, you know this is better," Petey said with a wide grin.

It seemed no time at all before they were entering the outskirts of University. The facilities were spread nearly all over town. In fact, the school *was* University. Rockwell explained that originally the town had been named something else, but the name had been changed to University when it was decided to locate the state's oldest educational institution there.

University was a typical small town. The houses possessed that quiet, peaceful air about their well-painted exteriors and neatly manicured landscaping. Here and there a sign outside a house proclaimed the home of a sorority or fraternity.

Rockwell parked near the big field house and sat quietly for several seconds. "All right," he began finally. "We're up here as guests of the university. I want you to enjoy every minute of it." He chuckled grimly. "And I want you to learn something! Don't be afraid to ask questions. Remember, these coaches up here are paid by the State Department of Education to teach youngsters like you all they can about athletics. Well, make them earn their money! Ask questions! Let's take something home with us besides a program."

CHAPTER 7

The Spring Festival

AFTER LUNCH, everyone assembled in the gymnasium. Chip studied the program. He wanted to see when Del Bennett, the university baseball coach, would be on the program. Bennett had been a major-league pitcher.

The president of the university was introduced and welcomed the high school athletes. He told them that University was proud to have them as its guests and hoped to serve them in years to come as students. He explained that the sports festival was held each spring right after the high school quarter examinations. Most of the college students had gone home for a brief vacation. Then the coaching staff was introduced.

Biggie shook his head in disbelief. "Can you imagine that?" he whispered. "Must be fifty of them!"

After the introductions, the director of athletics explained the program, and then everyone headed for the field house and the first session. Biggie and Taps Browning

STRIKE THREE!

gazed around in amazement. Three Valley Falls football fields could easily fit on the ground floor of the building!

Right after the baseball lectures, Chip slipped away from his group and caught up with Coach Bennett. "Mr. Bennett," he began, "could I please ask you a couple of questions about pitching?"

Coach Del Bennett smiled as he studied the embarrassed boy. "Why, you sure can! That's what I'm here for! Shoot!"

Chip explained that he had always wanted to be a pitcher and he'd like to know just what he should practice.

"What's your name? Hilton! You're not from Valley Falls, by any chance, are you?"

"Yes, sir!"

"But I thought you were a catcher, son. Weren't you up here last year?"

Chip explained that he had caught last year and was being used as a catcher this year, but his accident had left his ankle a little stiff, and he thought he might be of more help to the team as a pitcher.

"I can throw hard, Mr. Bennett," he said.

"There's a lot more to pitching than throwing a hard ball, young man. That's the trouble with most teenagers. Every kid who can throw hard thinks he ought to be a pitcher. I'll admit it's a good thing to start with, but there's a lot more to it. What does Coach Rockwell think about you as a pitcher?"

"Well, he . . . he doesn't know I want to be a pitcher, yet," Chip admitted hesitantly. "I thought I'd practice the right skills before I told him."

Bennett appraised the tall boy carefully. "You've got the right spirit. Tell you what I'll do. You meet me here tomorrow morning at eight o'clock, and I'll work with you until nine. Bring a catcher with you!"

THE SPRING FESTIVAL

Chip was walking on air when he rejoined Speed, Biggie, and Taps at the track demonstration. He whispered what had happened, and they all promised to accompany him in the morning.

Chip was up at 6:30 sharp the next morning. He had a little trouble with his friends.

"No, Chip," pleaded Speed, "just another half hour."

"None of that!" Chip said firmly.

"You don't have to meet Bennett until eight o'clock," Biggie protested. "What's the rush?"

"No rush!" Chip said. "Just want to be on time!"

It was ten minutes to eight when the four boys arrived at the big field house. There wasn't a person in sight.

"Suppose he doesn't show?" Speed began.

"He'll show up!" Chip said firmly.

Seconds later, Coach Bennett swung around the corner to find four alert young athletes waiting for him. He looked the four boys over carefully. He had heard of them; he hoped to see a lot more of them someday—at State!

Del Bennett was a big man in baseball; he had won many honors in the years he had pitched professional baseball, but his greatest honor had come from the Baseball Sportswriters of America who had elected him to the Hall of Fame. Bennett knew kids too; that was his business. He had a way with the boys who played under his direction. He treated them with respect, kindness, and understanding. He studied the four boys standing awkwardly before him.

"So this is the Valley Falls outfit?" He gave each boy a friendly smile and a firm clasp of the hand. "The Big Reds seem to be doing pretty well this year—state championship in football, state championship in basketball, and now, I suppose, you're aiming for the baseball pennant!"

But Bennett wasn't going to get much in the line of talk from this crew. They waited patiently but added nothing to the conversation. Bennett smiled.

"I get it!" he said, nodding his head understandingly. "Time's a-wasting and we're burning daylight! All right, let's go! We'll walk up to my office and grab a couple of gloves and work out right here in the field house with one of the indoor practice pitching setups."

Bennett was a tall man with muscle padding where it belonged. He moved swiftly and purposefully, yet his progress was so smooth and effortless that the boys would never have realized how fast he walked until they tried to keep up with him. Chip flashed a look of surprise at Speed as they tried to match the renowned coach's long strides.

A few minutes later, Chip, Biggie, and Taps stood near the pitching rubber listening to Coach Bennett. Speed waited behind the practice home plate thumping a big catcher's glove.

"Now, Hilton, the most important help to a pitcher is the catcher. I guess I don't have to go into that since you're a catcher, and a pretty good one, from what I hear. But a catcher can make or break a pitcher. Catchers are supposed to know a lot about hitters, to have a good memory, to know what a batter likes and dislikes, and what the pitcher can throw that will get the batter in a hole. He knows when to slow down a flighty pitcher, when to call for a waste pitch or a throw to a base, and how to control his battery mate's weaknesses.

"But enough of that. I simply brought that in to impress you with the importance to the team for a catcher and a pitcher to work together. Failure to work together means failure for the pitcher and the receiver as well."

Chip shifted his eyes slightly and met Biggie's understanding glance. Both boys were thinking of Nick Trullo.

THE SPRING FESTIVAL

"Now for pitching! We'll start with the ball. I myself always try to hold a ball so my first and second fingers rest across the seams. That's because I throw overhand all the time. Here, just shift that ball around in your hand, but end up each time feeling the seams with your thumb and two fingers. But before we go any further, let's see you throw a few." He handed Chip the ball.

Chip, a little self-conscious, threw the ball with plenty of zip into the glove Speed was holding as a target.

The coach watched the earnest young hurler for a moment and then he put his hand on Chip's shoulder.

"Hold up a minute, Hilton. You've got a pretty good sidearm motion there. Maybe you can develop that sidearm toss into your best pitch. In that case, you must grip the ball so that your first and second fingers each rest across the seams.

"That's enough about gripping the ball. The next thing is to be sure the ball is kept concealed from the batter until it is actually released from the pitching hand. You hide the ball with your glove, your body, and the leg you hoist in the air—in your case, since you're a right-hander—your left leg.

"Now, your stance. The pivot foot, that'll be *your* right foot, must be in contact with the rubber, but your weight is on your left, which is slightly behind the rubber.

"When you start your windup, your weight shifts slightly from your left to your right and back again, but when you throw the ball, it's all on your pivot foot. Then you follow through." Bennett looked Chip over carefully.

"You're tall," he said, "almost have my build—except for the spare tire. Take a long stride when you throw, but be sure to get your body around almost immediately with your glove in position so you will be in a proper fielding position."

STRIKE THREE!

In a few minutes, Chip was toeing the practice rubber under the watchful eyes of the expert teacher. Bennett stopped him again and again. *Every little detail has to be just right with this man,* Chip was thinking. *He's almost as bad as the Rock.*

"Control is the starting place for a youngster or an experienced big leaguer," Bennett continued softly. "Work on your control, Hilton, until you can 'thread a needle' with your fastball and your curveball! Then you'll be on your way to being a pitcher. After you can put that apple wherever you want it nine times out of ten, then it's time enough to work on some sort of change-of-pace pitch. A wild pitcher often gets himself out of a lot of jams because of his very wildness. Batters are afraid to take a toehold up there at the plate. But, in the long run, he doesn't last. A good pitcher *must* have control. There always comes a time in any ball game, you know, when the ball just has to cut that plate!

"I'll show you how I hold the ball for a knuckler, a slider, a screwball, and a forkball," he chuckled. "Not that you're ready for those, but it will give you the idea of the different throws pitchers sometimes master." He chuckled again. "I said *sometimes!* Most rookie pitchers who try to master a lot of stuff master none!

"The fastball remains the most effective pitch for a young hurler like you. I recommend you work on the three basic pitches: fastball, curveball, and a change-up."

For another half hour, Coach Bennett worked on Chip's pitching form and delivery. Finally, he breathed a sigh of satisfaction.

"You're ready to pitch right now, kid," he said with a smile. "All you need is a little experience. That, and a little more control of your curve."

Del Bennett looked at each boy and said, "A pitcher's

greatest success comes when he realizes and appreciates the efforts and contributions of his teammates. Looks like Coach Rockwell has done a fine job with you boys.

"Now, one last word. Keep the ball hidden at all times. Bring that long left leg of yours up high, and when you drive the ball toward the plate, finish with a long step and then into your fielding position. You throw hard enough, all right, but if you rely entirely on speed, the batters are going to gradually get their eyes and their timing speeded up, and then they'll begin to tee off. It'll be off to the showers for that pitcher!

"You've got to keep a batter off balance—a hard one, a soft one, something different, then a fast one inside. Get it? OK! Good luck. You can do it!"

From that time on, the trip to the university was meaningless as far as Chip Hilton was concerned. The basketball workout, the baseball game, and the football game, which followed that afternoon, just delayed his opportunity to get home to practice all the things he had learned from the legendary Hall of Famer.

Chip was up early Sunday morning. At the breakfast table before church, he relived the weekend for his mother. He was enthusiastic about Bennett's pitching instructions.

"He said I was a good high school pitcher right now, Mom. Guess the backyard practice is paying off!"

Right after lunch Soapy Smith showed up, and the two boys made a beeline for the backyard. Chip couldn't wait to try out his new knowledge and skills, and Soapy was just as eager to add all the information to his pursuit of catching. Taps Browning soon came bounding over the fence, and then Speed, Biggie, and Abe Cohen dropped in. That afternoon was one of the liveliest in the history of the Hilton A. C.

CHAPTER 8

Inside Baseball

BASEBALL HAS a way of working itself into the blood of players and fans alike. As the opening day drew near, each evening added a few more spectators in the Valley Falls High School stands. The players became more intense in their drive for positions, and the coaches worked even more feverishly to develop team play.

On Monday, the coaching staff began focusing on some of the finer points of the game. Stewart and Thomas worked with the outfielders while Rockwell gathered the infielders and the rest of the squad around him in front of home plate and began firing questions.

"What's the proper fielding position for a grass cutter, Morris? Ball coming straight at you!"

"Well, Coach, the first thing I do is get my eyes on the ball and keep watching it right into my glove. I try to meet the ball instead of waiting for it. I keep my body low, in a crouch, and I get my glove and my right hand down as close to the ground as possible."

"Good! How about the position of the feet?"

"*You* teach us to play the ball off the right leg, Coach, so we can pivot and achieve a better throwing position."

Rockwell nodded in satisfaction. "What comes before all that?"

Speed studied the ground a moment. "Guess you mean we should have the play all figured out before the pitcher throws the ball." Speed's face relaxed as Rockwell nodded.

"Right!" Rockwell shook a finger around the little circle. "I want every player—every player—to have *his* play figured out *before* the pitcher throws to the batter."

"How do you field a ball to your right, Collins?"

"Same way, Coach, except we slide our feet something like a basketball player does on the defense. I think it's called a crow-hop."

Rockwell nodded, "Good," and then asked, "Why?"

"That keeps us in a position to throw."

"Right! What if the ball is hit to your left?"

"You tell us to run toward the ball in that case, Coach."

"Why?"

"Because, when we run or move to our left, we're facing the first baseman and it's a natural throwing position. Of course, we can cover more ground when we run."

"How about a bounding ball, Badger?" The stocky third baseman thumped a fist into his glove several times before answering. "You're supposed to field that kind of ball at the top of the bounce, Coach," he said, "and you've got to keep your body squarely in front of the ball."

STRIKE THREE!

"How should a third baseman field a bunt or a slow hit ball?"

"Well, seems to me that's about the toughest play I have, Coach—"

Rockwell interrupted, "That's about the toughest play *any* third baseman has, Chris. Go ahead!"

"I'm supposed to come in on the run and pick the ball up with my bare hand and fire it over to first with a sidearm motion."

"How about tagging a runner, Collins?"

"We're supposed to take the throw so we can straddle the bag, Coach. Then, we hold the ball low in front of the base and let the runner slide into it."

"Why straddle the bag, Cody?"

"So we're ready for any kind of slide, Coach. Right or left or head on."

"What about throwing, Cohen?"

"An infielder should throw a ball with one continuous motion, Coach. If there's time, a player ought to throw overhand. But if the runner is fast, the ball should be snapped sidearm. You have to watch these throws, though, 'cause they curve from the inside out, especially if you are charging in to meet a slow roller."

"Right! Good! Now we'll have some situations. Smith, Leonard, and Carey here will take positions on the bases according to the play I want.

"I'll give you the score, the out, and the count on the hitter. We'll assume the batter is a right-handed hitter unless I tell you otherwise. Chip will flash the pitch the hurler is going to use to Morris, and Speed will pass it on to the infield. He'll also signal the pitch to the left fielder.

"Collins will take the signal from Morris and pass it on to the center and right fielders. Same signs we talked about in the strategy sessions. OK?"

INSIDE BASEBALL

The infielders dashed out on the field, and Chip pegged the ball down to Biggie on first. "Round the horn, guys," he yelled. "Round the horn!"

Rockwell sent Trullo and Peters out to the mound and told them to alternate on the plays. Then he called to Stewart that he was ready for the outfielders. Williams ran to his position in left field, Red Schwartz dashed out to center, and Mike Rodriguez moved over in right. Soapy Smith, Robby Leonard, and Carl Carey took positions behind the infield in back of first, second, and third. When all the players were in position, Rockwell called out the play and the situation.

"Bases loaded! Two down! Count's two and one!"

Rockwell then whispered something to Chip, who crouched and gave the sign for a curve. The coach sent a grass cutter sizzling down the third-base line. But Badger was ready! He had caught the sign from Speed that a right-handed batter was being fed a curve, and Chris was ready for a hit to his right. He hadn't moved, though, until Rockwell had actually hit the ball. Then Chris had moved to his right, fielded the ball smoothly, and easily beat Peters to the bag for a force play and the third out. Behind him, Speed Morris and Ted Williams backed up the play in their respective positions.

Rockwell called play after play, and Chip continued to give Speed the signs for the pitches. Chip and Speed had practiced this in the Hilton A. C. hundreds of times; they had this part of inside baseball down pat. In fact, they had two sets of signs they could interchange to confuse their opponents when they suspected the other team of stealing their signs. Rockwell had given these to the team the previous year, and Chip and Speed knew them by heart.

Everything was running smoothly. The lines in Rockwell's sun-tanned face relaxed, and small crinkles at the corner of his lips suggested a smile. The infield play was working like a clock. Cody Collins at the keystone bag and Chris Badger on the hot corner were beautifully in sync with Speed and Biggie.

Chip felt almost like his old self. But inwardly he wondered what was going to happen Saturday if he had to catch Trullo and the big left-hander refused to pay attention to the signs. What good would signs be if Trullo wouldn't throw the corresponding pitch?

After practice, Chip maneuvered his path toward the locker room so he walked with Chris Badger and Cody Collins. "What's the score on Nick, Cody?" he asked.

"Nick? What do you mean, Chip?"

"He's angry at me for some reason. I can't figure it out."

Cody looked thoughtfully at Chip. "Well," he said slowly, "Nick and Carl are pretty good friends, Chip, and they've been playing ball together for a long time."

"I know, Cody, but there's room on the team for two catchers. Just because I caught all the games last year doesn't mean I will this year. There just wasn't any other catcher last year. That's the reason the coach took me off first base." Chip paused and then continued with a wry smile, "Not that it mattered. Biggie's a better first baseman than I'd ever be. Besides, he's a lefty! I wish Nick and I could get things straightened out though."

Badger nodded understandingly. "It's tough, Chip," he said, "but Nick's stubborn. When he gets something in his head, it's pretty hard to get it out. Right now, he's mad because he heard you say there weren't any pitchers on this year's team. Besides, he wants Carl to beat you out for the regular catching job."

"But I didn't even *know* Nick was a pitcher," Chip protested worriedly. "I was talking about the players we had back from last year. As far as the catching job is concerned, Carl can have it if he can beat me out!"

"Carl's not in your class, Chip," Collins said firmly. "He can't beat you out unless your leg goes bad again!"

Badger took hold of Chip's arm. "I'd like to help you get straightened out with Nick, but I don't think it's possible. Maybe I shouldn't say this, but Nick and Carl hang out with some pretty tough guys up on the Hill. Not that Cody and I are too good for any of the crew up there, but . . . I guess you get what I mean."

Chip nodded and gave his two South Side friends a grateful smile.

Friday's practice was the best of the week. Rockwell really went all out! He started with the offensive and defensive signs. Rockwell told the catchers, Hilton and Carey, that one finger would be used for a fastball, two fingers for a curve, three fingers for a change-up or slow ball, wiggling fingers for a pitchout, and a clenched fist as a sign for the pitcher to throw to a base for a pickoff. The clenched fist was to be followed by one finger if the throw was to first base, two fingers for a throw to second, or three fingers for a throw to third.

"Remember," he cautioned, "you can adjust these signs any way you wish. If you think men on base are stealing your signs, you can use the second sign flashed as the sign for the real pitch. If necessary, you can even make it the third sign.

"I know some of you are thinking these signs are simple. Well, they are. But they're not too simple for the big leagues!"

He paused and regarded Soapy Smith as if he expected the comic to say something. But Soapy was concentrating. He couldn't afford a wisecrack when the coach was talking about catching. His heart was set on being ready for the day when Chip Hilton and Soapy Smith would form Valley Falls's number-one battery.

The first- and third-base coaches were next on the list.

"Smith," Rockwell said, "I want you to master the offensive signs like a book. You'll coach at third base tomorrow. That's the most important coaching job there is! In the event you are used in the game, Chet will take your place. The catcher who isn't in the lineup will do the coaching at first base. Coach Thomas will fill in there if he has to. I like to see kids out there in those coaching boxes though. It's a good education. Some of you may even become coaches one day!

"Now, get this! Third-base coach gives the signs to left-hand hitters. First-base coach gives them to the right-hand hitters."

Rockwell then lashed into the hitters. "Unless I send a hitter into the batter's box 'on his own,' he must watch the coach before every pitch. Stay out of that batter's box until you've got the sign and everyone in on the play has acknowledged it. Get it? Any questions?

"Now! Hit-and-run plays! Remember, the sign will come from the bench to the coaches, from the coaches to the batter, and from the batter to the runner or runners. The runner or runners must acknowledge the signs too.

"For tomorrow, all batting and base-running signs will be given while moving. Base runners will acknowledge by tipping their hats while they are *moving!* Get it? *Moving!* Moving the body by bending down or sideways or backward, or by moving the feet—taking a step or a short run. Batters will be moving when they give the signals, and so will the coaches.

"Now, remember! We give signals all the time—standing still *or* moving. But the signs given while moving will be the ones that are on.

"You batters! On a hit-and-run, you've got to try to hit the ball on the ground. Even if it's a pitchout, swing at it! That helps the runner! If you miss a sign, step out of the box.

"Pay attention to this! When the count is three and two, the batter is on his own!"

There was a deep silence as Rockwell paused and glanced at the alert ring of faces. What he saw must have pleased him, for the determined bulging in his jaw slackened.

"Remember, high school games are seven innings according to our state athletic association. We'll play extra innings as long as needed, or until the umpire stops the game due to darkness. You're a good team," he said. "Good enough to become state champs if you pull together."

Chip shifted his eyes to Trullo's face, but Nick continued gazing intently at the ground.

"Now, one last word! We'll elect a captain tomorrow just before game time. Think about your leader tonight, and pick a good one tomorrow afternoon. That's all! Two laps and hit the showers!"

CHAPTER 9

Hit the Dirt

"ALL RIGHT, come on! Let's go!" Chet Stewart urged from the steps leading to the gym. "Hurry up! We've got to elect a captain today and get going!"

Chip was having trouble tugging his baseball pants over the ankle Pop Brown had carefully taped, but he caught Speed's glance and winked. He nodded his head toward Ted Williams and grinned. Chip, Speed, and Biggie had planned this election for a long time. Ted was going to end Valley Falls athletics after this season; this would be his last year in sports before going to college. It was only right, his three friends reasoned, that he should captain his last high school team.

The squad was soon assembled upstairs in the gym, each player holding his baseball shoes in his hands. Chip's thoughts went back to last September when he and Speed had been elected co-captains of the football team. Today, he didn't have the same tightness in his throat he'd had then.

HIT THE DIRT

Ted Williams, a popular choice, was elected unanimously. The players drowned his protests with cheers that filled the big gym. Rockwell shook Ted's hand warmly and congratulated the team on its choice.

"Ted will make a fine captain for you," Rock said. "Let's give him a good team to lead!"

On the field they found Paddy Jackson, dressed in a baseball uniform at least three sizes too large, jealously guarding the row of bats in front of the home dugout. Petey had bought the suit for Paddy, and it was complete even to the Valley Falls inscription across the jersey.

Paddy was as proud as could be. His freckled face was scrubbed clean, and just a wisp of his red hair protruded from under the bill of his cap. Paddy had worked hard all week getting ready for this day. He already knew the bats everyone on the team used.

The day was perfect for baseball—the kind of early spring day that promises a long, lazy summer. Virtually no wind blew, and the sun was warm as toast. The opening-game crowd was spirited. Fans were taking advantage of the pleasant day to get outdoors, and they wanted to see what sort of ball club the coach was going to unveil.

Rockwell had not said who would pitch. He'd make his decision when the team took fielding practice. Chip knew the Rock though. He had probably made up his mind a long time ago.

Chip envied the pitchers who were warming up. As he returned the ball to Peters, he began to analyze each of the moundsmen.

Little Lefty Peters was an expert with the soft stuff. He could bend a ball around a barrel, but he had no speed and tired quickly.

Nick Trullo, another lefty, was strong and loose. So far, he seemed to be the answer to Rockwell's pitching problem. A high school team didn't have to have a lot of pitchers. The games were usually four or five days apart, sometimes a whole week. It was not unusual for one pitcher to work nearly all the games during a season.

Before fielding practice, Rockwell summoned the squad and announced the lineup.

"We'll bat in this order: Rodriguez, right field, leading off; Collins, second base, batting second; Morris, shortstop, third; Williams, left field, fourth . . ."

Chip held his breath. He had alternated between the cleanup spot and fifth all the previous season.

"Cohen, first base, fifth—"

Chip's heart sank. But still . . . maybe.

"Schwartz, center field, sixth; Badger, third base, seventh—"

Two more, and catchers usually batted in the eighth spot.

"Hilton, catcher, eighth; Peters, pitcher, last! Let's go!"

They broke from the circle and scampered onto the field, clapping hands and pepping it up. Rockwell began hitting grounders to the infield, and Bill Thomas lifted long flies to the boys out by the fences.

Chet Stewart had Carl Carey and Soapy Smith in a huddle.

"Coach said you should take the third-base coaching box, Soapy. Remember, you give the left-handed hitters their signs. You take first-base coaching, Carl, and give the signs to right-handed hitters.

"Get this, both of you! All signs come from the bench. Coach gives them himself from the side of the dugout next to home plate. The only Weston guys who can possibly see them are out on the field, and they'll be too busy to try to steal bench signs.

HIT THE DIRT

"One more thing! Everything's off when the coach takes off his cap. Then you do the same thing, according to what the hitter is. If he's a lefty, it'll be you, Soapy; if he's a right-hander, you do it, Carl. OK?"

Accompanied by scattered cries of "Here comes the ump!" the umpire walked out to announce the batteries.

"For Weston, Parsons and Miller. For Valley Falls, Peters and Hilton. P-L-A-Y B-A-L-L!"

The Big Reds charged onto the field accompanied by the crowd's cheers and applause. The warm-up ball whipped around the field with bulletlike precision. From first base, Biggie drilled the ball back to Chip, who had moved out in front of home plate. Chip tossed the ball to Peters at the mound, trotted back behind the plate, and pulled on his mask. The game was on!

Weston was a weak-hitting club. That was apparent right away as Peters struck out the first three men to face him. But there Weston's weakness ended. It was a strong team in the field, especially with Parsons on the mound. He was a senior, and Chip remembered him from the previous year. Parsons was a good pitcher, and if he was in form, the Big Reds would have trouble. He got off to a good start in his half of the first inning, striking out Rodriguez and Collins, walking Morris, and forcing Ted Williams to pop up weakly to the catcher. Parsons was like the season—too far ahead of the hitters.

Neither team scored until the last half of the fourth when Chip, batting left-handed, led off and singled sharply to right field. Peters laid a neat bunt down along the first-base line but was thrown out at first. Parsons was on top of the ball like a pouncing cat, but there wasn't time for a double play. Chip was away with the pitch and reached second base almost as soon as Parsons fielded the ball.

STRIKE THREE!

Mike Rodriguez walked, and Cody Collins, hitting right-handed, came to bat with a chance to put the Big Reds out in front. He was late on his swing, but it was a perfect hit over the first baseman's head. The ball cut out toward the right-field fence just inside the white chalk mark. Chip, on his way with the crack of the bat, went all the way to score the first run of the game standing up. Cody slid into second, but it wasn't necessary. The throw was to the plate. Soapy held Rodriguez on third.

Parsons walked Morris again, and the bases were loaded with one away and Williams up. But Parsons had Ted's number. He teased the eager captain with two benders and then whizzed a third strike right past the Big Reds captain's wrist. Biggie Cohen, on deck, had been swinging four bats. Now he took a firm toehold in the batter's box and stood poised with his big bat perfectly still.

Parsons knew Cohen. He wasn't going to give the big batter a good ball, and the duel between the two was pretty to watch. But Biggie looked them over carefully and finally walked. Rodriguez was forced in for a run, and the bases were still loaded with two away.

Red Schwartz was up. Red had a good eye; he had been one of the best shots on the hoops squad. Parsons tried to work him with balls just outside the strike zone, but Schwartz wouldn't bite. Red waited Parsons out and, when the count reached three and two, punched the "fat" pitch into left field. He tore down to second when a play was made on Cohen at third. Speed was right on Cody Collins's heels when the pair of them scored. So it was four runs, two outs, second and third bases occupied, and Chris Badger at bat.

The Weston captain called time and was joined by the Weston coach in a huddle around Parsons. They were evidently discussing the advisability of walking Badger so a play could be made at any base. Chip was on deck, swinging three bats. He saw them looking his way. The huddle broke up, and Parsons began to pitch to Badger. They had evidently decided against an intentional pass.

Chip felt a little pleased about that. No matter how bad he looked behind the plate, he reflected, his hitting ability was still respected.

Parsons worked on Badger skillfully and finally got Chris to go for one low and inside. Badger got a piece of the ball but was an easy out from Parsons to first. The score: Valley Falls 4, Weston 0.

The small visiting crowd took the between-innings stretch while the Big Reds were taking the field. Chip studied Lefty Peters. The Weston hitters were beginning to time their swings, and the little pitcher had no fastball to balance his slow stuff. In addition, Chip sensed that Lefty was beginning to tire. He cast a speculative eye toward Rockwell. Trullo was still in the dugout. He and Carl Carey were sitting together, watching every move Chip made, openly critical and antagonistic.

Chip could hear several raucous voices badgering Rockwell from the home stands, but he didn't recognize the voices. He forgot them immediately because Lefty suddenly began to flounder and walked the first two men!

Chip called time and was joined by Rockwell in front of the mound. "Are you tired, Lefty?" Rockwell asked with concern. "If you are, don't be afraid to say so. Trullo is ready."

But Lefty pleaded for a chance to finish the inning, and Rockwell decided to go along with him. Chip was sure the Rock knew Lefty was tiring. Why didn't the coach lift him? Then Rockwell's position struck him. If the coach put Trullo in and the big southpaw went bad, there'd be no other pitcher available. That was it.

Rockwell left Peters on the mound. The home fans loudly protested his decision. Lefty was having trouble controlling his slow curve and hit a batter to fill the bases. The next batter topped a dribbler along the third-base line, but Chris Badger made a bare-handed scoop and shot the ball underhand to Chip for a home-plate force-out. But the bases were still loaded, and the home crowd was growing louder in disapproval.

"Wake up, Rockwell! Take him out!"

"Put Trullo and Carey in there!"

"What are you savin' Trullo for? The prom?"

"We want Trullo!"

Rockwell sent Carey and Trullo out in front of the home bleachers to warm up, but Lefty stayed on the mound. Then, with the Big Reds infield playing in, the Weston cleanup batter met one on the nose, and the ball streaked along the ground far to Biggie Cohen's right.

Chip threw off his mask and crouched in front of the plate, but he groaned aloud when he saw Biggie was going to be out of position for a throw to the plate even if he managed to stop the ball. The runner from third came in, and the man from second tore around the hot corner and headed for the plate.

Biggie stabbed at the ball with his gloved right hand and got it. He pivoted and tossed the ball with the same hand to Speed. The runner coming into second tried to take Morris out in an effort to save the third out at first base. Speed's foot stabbed the inside corner of the bag just as he took Biggie's toss. A split second later, Speed was hit by the diving Westonian, but he threw the ball toward first base before he tumbled down on top of the runner.

Chip shifted his eyes toward first. Lefty Peters was streaking for the bag almost on a line with the batter. Speed's throw was ahead of Peters, but the speeding pitcher spread-eagled and tagged the bag just as the ball landed in his frantically outstretched hand. The runner hit Lefty at the same time, and the two boys crashed behind first base.

Chip barely glanced at the second Weston runner to come tearing into home; he was watching Lefty and the base umpire. The umpire jerked his thumb in the air. Lefty was lying on the ground clutching the ball; his one-hand catch had completed the double play.

The fans were screaming and jumping with excitement.

"What a play! Neither run counts!"

"They were both hit!"

"Did you ever see such a stop!"

"Peters is hurt! And so is Morris!"

They were both hurt, all right. Lefty was limping badly, and Rockwell headed him for the gym in spite of the little pitcher's protests.

"It's about time!" someone bellowed from behind the home dugout. Chip glanced up and met the angry glare of Buck Adams. Adams was sitting next to Peck Weaver, and both were bitter in their abuse of Rockwell.

Speed Morris was accustomed to hard spills. The flashy shortstop was an All-State halfback and had been a marked man in every football game. Speed knew how to walk off a bad fall.

Trullo began throwing to Chet Stewart, and Carl Carey took Peters's place on deck. Chip unsnapped his shin guards and slipped the chest protector over his head. He was up.

As he started for the bat rack, Paddy came running with Chip's favorite bat. Paddy kissed the bat near the heavy end. "Smack it right there, Chip," he begged.

Chip knocked some imaginary mud from his spikes and swung the bat several times. Parsons was fast; he was a right-hander too, which pleased Chip. Although he was a switch hitter, Chip liked to hit left-handed best; he was a long stride nearer first base, and when he swung through, his pivot turned him toward first and threw him into high gear almost with the crack of the bat. He could watch right-handed pitches almost to the bat, too, it seemed.

Parsons eyed the tall catcher appraisingly. He wanted to strike this bothersome Big Red out. So far, Hilton was two for two. Parsons sneaked the first one through for a called strike. Chip liked to take one and made no attempt to go after it. Parsons tried coaxing Chip with an outside pitch, but Hilton's keen eye was waiting for the good ones. After two low, inside pitches went by for balls, the count was three and one. Then Chip dug in.

Parsons curved the next one, but it didn't break soon enough, and Chip met the ball solidly, punching it to his left. It landed just beyond the third baseman and just inside the left-field foul line. Chip knew he had hit it hard and decided to stretch it into a double if at all possible. As he sped toward first, he watched Carey. But Carl gave him no sign, and Chip realized he'd get no help here.

He rounded the bag and continued at full speed for second base. Ahead of him, the Weston left fielder set himself for the throw, and from the position of the second baseman covering the bag, Chip knew he'd have to slide in with his bad ankle. He would have to hit the dirt!

Soapy, in the third-base coaching box, was yelling frantically, "Stay up! Stay up!"

But Chip wasn't that kind of player. A real ballplayer *always* hits the dirt on a close play. Chip never slackened speed but hurled his legs and body in a half-twist and jammed his injured left leg into the bag. He felt the bag a split second before the tag. Through the dust he turned his head to see the base umpire's hands wide, palms down.

"Safe!"

Then he felt the pain. It was running up his leg like a tongue of fire.

CHAPTER 10

One for All

"SAFE?" SCREAMED the Weston second baseman. "Safe? I had him by a mile! You blind?"

"No!" bellowed the umpire. "No, I'm not blind! Young man, if you want to stay in this ball game, you'd better quit talking and start walking! You get over there where you belong and stay there!"

The short interruption gave Chip a chance to test his ankle. Little by little he shifted his weight to the aching leg. The pain was paralyzing. He knew he should try to walk it off, but he knew, too, that the Rock's keen, black eyes would be watching every step he made. The Rock would yank him the second he thought he was hurt.

When play resumed, Chip managed a few steps off the bag. Soapy was watching him closely. "I'll take the infielders, Chip," Soapy kept chanting. "You watch the pitcher. There he goes! Watch out! He'll steal your glove."

STRIKE THREE!

But Parsons was concentrating on the batters. He was peeved and used only twelve pitches to strike out Carey, Rodriguez, and Collins. Chip kept moving around, but it took all his self-control to disguise his ankle injury on the way to the dugout. He was worried about Rockwell's next substitution. Carey had batted for Lefty Peters. Did that mean Rock would put Trullo in for Chip Hilton?

Soapy helped Chip get into his catching gear, and Rockwell called Trullo. He talked to the big southpaw a few seconds and then told him he was replacing Carey. Chip's heart leaped. Now he *had* to finish this game; Carey couldn't go back in the game. Of course, there was Soapy Smith, but Rock didn't know about Soapy. In spite of himself, Chip couldn't help wishing someday Rockwell would put him on the mound with Soapy behind the plate.

Pain after pain shot up his leg now, and while he took Trullo's warm-up pitches, he tried desperately to put the ache out of his mind. He carried the ball out to the mound and gave Trullo the signs. Nick sullenly looked away and kept slapping the ball into his glove but said nothing. Chip walked slowly back to the plate and squatted behind the hitter.

Trullo walked the first man and hit the next, putting runners on first and second with none out. He was wild, but there was something else wrong. Chip called time and again walked out to the box.

"Come on, Nick," he said, "settle down!" He plunked the ball into his glove several times before continuing. "You getting my signs all right?"

Trullo barely glanced at Chip. "Yeah, sure," he growled.

Chip's gray eyes narrowed a bit as he searched Trullo's face. "You must have them mixed up then, Nick," he said slowly. "One finger is for your fastball, two means your curve, and three is for your change—"

Trullo reached out and grabbed the ball. "Get back in your cage, Hilton," he said. "You do the catching. I'll do the pitching!" Nick deliberately turned his back on Chip, walked behind the pitcher's rubber, and picked up the little rosin bag from the ground.

Chip didn't move. He stood there patiently until Trullo faced around. "All right, Nick," he said softly, "you pitch 'em! I'll catch 'em!"

Trullo pitched and Chip caught—most of them. Chip gave what he considered the correct sign and then waited uncertainly for the pitch; he was just as unprepared as the batter for the throw. Trullo put on a good act though. He looked down the alley at Chip as if they were working together. Several times he went so far as to pretend to shake off a sign.

Chip was boiling. His ankle pained him every time he moved, but he didn't dare relax because he was in the dark on every pitch Trullo made. Inside, he was seething. In the practice games he had overlooked Trullo's refusal to throw the correct pitch, but this was a real game. This counted!

The third batter plopped a short bunt a little distance in front of the plate and toward first base. Chip swept off his mask and tore after the ball. Trullo came charging in too. Chip yelled, "Mine!" but Nick never stopped. Just as Chip's hand closed over the ball, Trullo's charge knocked them both to the ground, and the ball spun out of Chip's hand. Chip scrambled to his feet and chased the ball clear to the backstop while two Weston runners dashed across the plate. The hitter went all the way to third.

Once again Chip called time. He didn't feel any pain now—only a burning anger that surged through him. He walked straight out to the mound where Trullo was viciously kicking the dirt.

"Listen, Trullo," Chip gritted through set teeth, "this has gone far enough! You pitch what I call from now on—understand! Another thing! When this game is over, I'm ready for a showdown with you anytime and anyplace you name. Right now, we've got a game to win. But remember what I said!"

But Valley Falls wasn't to win that game. Weston tied up the score immediately, and Parsons, pitching for all he was worth, held the Big Reds in their half of the sixth.

In the top of the seventh, with a man on third, two away, and two strikes on the batter, Trullo crossed Chip up with a terrific bender that hooked around the hitter's ankles and got away. Chip couldn't even get his glove on the ball. The batter missed the ball, but when it got away from Chip, he sprinted for first base. The man on third scored, putting Weston out in front for the first time during the game.

It wasn't important that Trullo struck out the next hitter, for Parsons stopped the Big Reds cold, setting Taylor, Morris, and Williams down one-two-three for the final outs of the game. The game was over. The score: Weston 5, Valley Falls 4. The Big Reds had lost their opening game to the weakest team in Section Two!

Chip stomped toward the gym, deliberately punishing his numb ankle. The silent dressing room was charged with tension. Chip's temper was at the breaking point. He didn't look at Trullo for fear he'd lose all control of himself.

Speed turned to Chip and studied him anxiously. "You and Nick got a new set of signs, Chip?" he asked. "I didn't get more than two or three of them all the time Nick was pitching!" His eyes flickered over to Biggie, but Cohen was looking straight ahead.

Soapy jumped to the point. "He crossed you up, didn't he, Chip?"

Chip deliberated. Now was the time to tell his three friends everything, but this thing had become a personal problem. He guessed he'd have to work it out on his own.

"No, Soapy," he said quietly. "I wasn't crossed up. I knew what to expect." He turned to Morris. "And we don't have a new set of signs, Speed. Nick just isn't set on the signs yet. They're new to him, you know."

"Yeah, sure, we know," Biggie Cohen said sourly.

After dinner, Chip headed straight for the Sugar Bowl and directly for the storeroom, where he waited impatiently for Doc Jones's arriving footsteps on the floor above. When he heard Jones moving about in his office, he hurried up the steps and charged into the office.

Doc Jones showed no surprise at Chip's abrupt entrance. "Old Patch-'Em-Up" looked calmly over his glasses at Chip and eased himself slowly into his chair. He hooked his thumbs in the armholes of his vest and regarded Chip with kindly eyes. "What's the trouble, Chipper?" he asked.

Chip recounted the afternoon's injury to his ankle. Little by little Doc Jones also wormed out of him something about his difficulty with Nick Trullo and the competition for the catcher's spot.

"He doesn't like me, Doc. This afternoon I let a ball get away from me and lost the game. It meant the winning run for Weston. Nick won't pay any attention to the signs and the whole team is upset—all because Carl Carey is sitting in the dugout, and Nick has to pitch to me. I don't know what to do about it!"

Doc Jones leaned back in his chair.

"Chip," he began slowly, "I guess most of your trouble has been my fault. I told the coach to hold you down for a month to give your leg a chance. The bump you got this afternoon means nothing. That ankle is stronger than the other one, but it's still tender. You'll probably get a lot of aches in that leg, but it's nothing to get alarmed about. Guess you can stand a little pain if it means you can play ball! Right?"

Jones paused. The little wrinkles that flanked his gray eyes bunched up a bit, and his mouth twisted up in a half-smile. Chip smiled a little too.

"One game doesn't make a season, Chip. Remember, Rockwell knows baseball and he knows teenagers. He'll take care of everything at the proper time. He might even try Carey behind the plate and let you sit the bench for a game or two." Jones let this sink in and then said, "He might even use you in the bull pen.

"You know, Chip, it's a very special kind of kid or man who can stay on his toes while sitting the bench. You proved that this past winter during the basketball season."

Chip's thoughts were racing. He was suddenly ashamed of all the personal grief he'd just dumped on Doc. The *team* was the thing! Not Chip Hilton. If Trullo was a good pitcher and wanted Carl Carey to be his catcher and it meant a successful season for Valley Falls, well, Chip Hilton could sit the bench or be a good pinch hitter. He'd play any place the Rock put him.

"You see, Chipper, you're used to being the star. At one time or another, every star has to play a supporting role. Maybe that's half your trouble. Maybe you aren't big enough to take a *little* part.

"The team's the thing, Chip. 'One for all and all for one' sounds like idealistic nonsense to a lot of people. But you can't laugh at that philosophy in sports, Chipper. No teamwork, no team!

"Suppose you just forget about the 'all for one' part and concentrate on the 'one for all.' See that Chip Hilton does what's best for the team. Then everything will come out all right!"

Chip got slowly to his feet. "Thanks, Doc," he said. "Guess most of my trouble was in the head. I've been thinking too much about Chip Hilton and not enough about the team!"

Late that night Doc Jones and John Schroeder took a long walk, and their steps, for some reason, carried them to the gate in front of Coach Rockwell's house.

The conversation of the three men was short and to the point—a point very important to Chip Hilton's baseball career!

CHAPTER 11

Play a Little Part

AFTER JOHN SCHROEDER and Doc Jones left, Coach Henry Rockwell sat alone in his study. He had been greatly disappointed in the results of the afternoon's game. His disappointment stemmed not so much because the Big Reds had lost the game but because of the way the loss had come about. He reviewed his number-one technical principle of the "straight line" from catcher through pitcher and second base to center field carefully, starting with Chip Hilton.

Hilton was a veteran receiver, the leading hitter the past season, and, undoubtedly, the best all-around athlete at Valley Falls High School. Chip had a powerful arm and threw well to every base. Besides, he was a student of baseball, and behind those steady, gray eyes was a mind that functioned brilliantly in any athletic situation. As a catcher, the boy measured each batter carefully, studying the hitter's stance, grip on the bat, and degree of confidence. Once a weakness was discovered, Chip could be counted on to work with his pitcher in playing the advantage to the hilt.

Trullo was the only pitcher who showed promise. The big, swarthy boy threw a hard ball and, if his wildness could be controlled, might develop into a fine pitcher. However, his attitude was bad. Trullo was sullen and, with the exception of Carl Carey, friendly with none of the other members of the team.

Rockwell reviewed the afternoon's game, inning by inning. Trullo had pitched the last few innings, and those were the frames when the game had been lost. Contributing factors were the passed balls and the collision between Trullo and Hilton, but he had sensed something else more important: several little byplays between the two boys clearly showed lack of harmony.

Perhaps he was wrong about Hilton. Maybe the ankle was strong enough, but Chip's ability to make sudden and unexpected moves might have been affected. The big kid had seldom been charged with a passed ball the previous year. That must be it. Rockwell decided to give Carl Carey a little more attention during the coming week.

But what to do with Hilton? He'd be a perfect pinch hitter! But it was a shame to shelve the kid's all-round baseball ability. Catching was the toughest job in baseball; maybe he could shift him to right field. That would give the team another strong-hitting regular who could concentrate on batting. But how about the pitching idea? John Schroeder and Doc Jones might have something there; maybe the kid *could* pitch!

Rockwell half-smiled to himself. It *would* be something if Chip Hilton turned out to be the pitcher Big Chip Hilton, so many years ago, had hoped his son would be.

STRIKE THREE!

Both had been first sackers, and Rockwell had converted each into a catcher.

Trullo and Peters were both southpaws. He could sure use a good right-hand hurler. Today's game might not have been lost if he could have shot a right-hander in there for those last several innings.

But how about the catching? Carey was inexperienced; he didn't know the subtleties and the little inside plays that made Chip so valuable behind the plate.

Later, when Rockwell finally went to bed, he had made up his mind to go along with Chip Hilton behind the plate for another week or so. He wasn't going to be stampeded into a change because of the loss of one game.

Just about the time John Schroeder and Doc Jones were leaving Rockwell, Petey Jackson checked in at the poolroom. Petey loved playing pool; it was about the only activity he could take on and make any kind of respectable showing. The poolroom was one place where Petey could show his supremacy over another person in real competition, and he was always the center of the show in Sorelli's. In addition, he was known for his intense loyalty to Rockwell and the Big Reds. The minute he entered the side door of Sorelli's, several of his hecklers began badgering him.

"What happened to the state champs? Looks like they're state chumps!"

"The Rock's rockheads got rocked today, didn't they?"

"You'd think Hilton was still playing football the way he kicked the ball around. And he booted my five bucks right out the window!"

"What's wrong with your hero, Jackson? Can't he handle a southpaw pitcher?"

PLAY A LITTLE PART

Petey was surrounded, but he tried his best. "Ya can't win 'em all," he protested.

"*All?*" someone shouted. "They'll be lucky to win *one!*"

Buck Adams waved a handful of money under Petey's nose. "As much of this as you want says they don't win next Friday's game! With Hilton tryin' to catch, they couldn't beat the South Side Juniors!"

Peck Weaver joined Adams. "I've got a hundred bucks here that says Parkton knocks 'em off next Friday! Want any part of it, soda jerkie?"

Petey backed up. He didn't want any part of gambling or arguments with Peck Weaver and Buck Adams. "No . . . no," he stammered, "I don't gamble."

Buck Adams laughed boisterously. "We don't either, soda boy. Gambling means takin' a chance! We don't take no chances! We got us a surefire system!"

"Yeah," added Weaver, "ole Leroy White handicaps them for us!"

Petey's two tormentors slapped each other on the back and turned toward the back of the room. Petey hurriedly got into a game and out of the discussion. As he searched for the kind of cue he liked, he breathed a sigh of relief, but he couldn't get Buck Adams and Peck Weaver out of his mind. Nor *Leroy White.*

Chip was awake early the next morning and, settling down in the porch swing, opened the Sunday *Post* to the sports section. His fears were realized. Pete Williams discussed in detail the gaff Chip and Nick Trullo had perpetrated in failing to field the booted bunt.

Although Chip Hilton had a perfect day at bat, three hits and a walk, his errors behind the plate and his handling of Trullo were atrocious.

STRIKE THREE!

Joe Kennedy of the *Times* charged Chip with an error on the passed ball and attributed the loss of the game to that play. He called the passed ball the sharpest breaking ball he had ever seen a "Big Reds pitcher pull the string on!" Kennedy praised Trullo's pitching and concluded Trullo and Hilton would make a great battery as soon as Hilton became familiar with Trullo's stuff.

Chip snorted. "Familiar with Trullo's stuff!" That was a laugh. The best catcher couldn't hold a pitcher unless he knew what to expect!

Chip mulled over the rumors he had heard. First, it had been Petey with stories of gambling on the high school baseball games. Yesterday, Biggie had told him some of the pottery men were losing their wages in a big-money baseball pool the South-Siders were backing at Sorelli's.

Why had Buck Adams and Peck Weaver been talking about him? What was Ken Carey's connection with Adams and Weaver? Could Nick Trullo and Carl Carey possibly be mixed up with Adams and Weaver?

Chip dismissed that thought almost as quickly as it crossed his mind. Trullo and Carl Carey might not like him personally and might be trying to show him up so they could team up together, but Chip couldn't believe they'd be mixed up with anything like that.

Soapy Smith appeared right after lunch, and the two boys practiced their pitching and catching in the backyard until Speed, Biggie, and Red Schwartz joined them. Until 3:30, when Chip had to start for the Sugar Bowl, all talk centered on the game. Chip sensed his friends were trying to smooth the way for him to explain the trouble with Nick Trullo, but he skillfully avoided all their attempts to draw him into that discussion.

PLAY A LITTLE PART

After Chip had gone to work, Soapy, Speed, Red, and Biggie discussed the situation. Something had to done, they all agreed. Red Schwartz was particularly bitter.

"How much longer we gonna take this?" he demanded. "What's the matter with Chip? He ought to bust that guy!"

Speed shrugged his shoulders. "You know how he is," he said. "You can't talk to him about it! One thing's sure; he'll take just so much from Trullo and that will be it!"

"In the meantime, we're supposed to go on losing games, I suppose!" Biggie Cohen said dryly. "Just because Chip's too good a sport to tell the coach about it."

"Someone ought to tell him!" Soapy said belligerently. "I feel like telling him the whole story myself."

"I don't know why Ted can't talk to the coach," said Speed slowly. "He's the captain, and that's the most important part of a captain's job—to represent the team and keep 'em hustling!"

Later, when things quieted down at the Sugar Bowl, Petey Jackson approached Chip, who was checking an invoice at Mr. Schroeder's desk.

"Got a minute, Chip?" asked Petey.

"Sure," replied Hilton, looking up.

Then Petey dramatically recounted his run-in with Buck Adams and Peck and their elation over their winnings. Chip listened apathetically. He just wasn't interested anymore in the fact that two South Side men had won money on a Big Reds baseball game. Nor was he interested in Petey's conjectures about Leroy White. Chip didn't care who Leroy White was! However, when Petey told Chip about Adams and Weaver's willingness to wager that Parkton would beat the Big Reds the coming

STRIKE THREE!

Friday, Chip suddenly came alive. He quizzed Petey thoroughly about their statements.

At home, Chip spent a long evening trying to piece together the puzzle confronting him. He couldn't get Buck Adams and Peck Weaver out of his mind. Why were they so confident Parkton would win on Friday?

His thoughts shifted back to the game, and he began to wonder what would happen at school tomorrow. "Blue Monday" was right, he reflected.

But the next day wasn't so bad after all. Kids have a way of forgetting a defeat, and everyone seemed to have forgotten the unfortunate result; interest centered on the upcoming game. As Speed often said, "Nothing is so dead as yesterday's news."

As soon as Chip reached the locker room that afternoon, Pop stopped him. "Come on up, Chip. The coach said he wanted to see you as soon as you showed up!"

Rockwell had been studying his baseball problem and reading a letter from Del Bennett, State's baseball coach. Now he fingered the letter and read it again.

STATE UNIVERSITY
April 21

Dear Rock,

Am writing you this letter, more or less off the record, about one of your kids by the name of Chip Hilton. The youngster asked me to give him some tips on pitching when you brought your athletes up here, and I worked out with him one morning.

The kid has a lot of stuff, Rock. He told me you didn't know anything about his desire to be a pitcher. He seemed all wrapped up in this throwing deal and didn't want to let you know about it until he was ready. Well, in my opinion, he's ready now. Don't know how you are fixed for pitchers, but if you're not too strong in that department, maybe you ought to give Hilton a try.

Regards,
Del

Rockwell sighed. Coaching had a lot of problems besides winning or losing games. Everyone wanted to get in on the show at one time or another about an athlete. Right now, the player was Chip Hilton. John Schroeder, Doc Jones, and now Del Bennett all wanted to tell him what position the kid should play.

Chip's knock on the door ended Rockwell's thoughts. After Chip was seated, Rockwell wasted no time.

"Chip, I know you feel low about Friday, so I'll tell you right now I didn't ask you up here to talk about the game. I do want to talk to you about your catching and about Nick Trullo.

"Last year, you were the All-State receiver. You could throw as well as any college catcher in the country, fielded your position without an error, and ran the team as a catcher should. This year, you haven't been picking runners off the bases; your throws to second have been late or not at all, and your catching and fielding have slipped. Why?"

Chip shook his head uncertainly but said nothing. He was thinking about some of the things Doc Jones had said about the team and about being big enough to play a little part.

STRIKE THREE!

"Now, Chip, I know you and Nick Trullo aren't clicking. Coach Stewart thinks part of the difficulty lies in the fact that Trullo and Carey are buddies and they want to work together. How about it?"

"Well, Coach," Chip said slowly, "I think that's got a lot to do with Nick's feelings toward me. I think Nick would work better with Carl because they know each other. They've worked a lot of games together—"

Rockwell interrupted him. "Chip, I'm not worrying at all about your ability as a catcher. Perhaps I am a bit worried about your ankle—" Rockwell checked Chip. "Now, just a minute. I know Doc Jones said it was all right, and I know you think it is too. But it may be just that it's stiff—needs more time and work. I said time and work, not rest!

"We'll just go along the way we are for another week, and in the meantime I'll look Carey over. Then we'll see about other things, like pinch hitting or—pitching."

CHAPTER 12

You Catch—
I'll Pitch!

FRIDAY WAS always a welcome day in high school. To some students it meant an end to classes, the approach of a pleasant weekend, spending time with friends, an exciting social event, or a late morning's sleep. To others it was an opportunity to earn extra money, the time to pursue a personal hobby, or a chance to participate in or watch a school game or performance. Chip fell into the last group. He was looking forward to the afternoon's game with Parkton. He wanted to redeem himself for the Weston debacle.

After his last class, Chip, Speed, and Biggie met in the gym foyer to purchase the *Yellow Jacket*. Chip turned to the sports page. There it was again, just as it had been for the past three weeks.

STRIKE THREE!

THE BATTING CAGE

WILL Coach Rockwell persist in losing games in order to keep Chip Hilton behind the plate? Wouldn't Chip be more valuable to the team as a pinch hitter?

WHO was responsible for the head-on collision between Trullo and Hilton?

ISN'T the catcher supposed to call all the plays in front of the plate? Weston's winning run was scored on a missed third strike *with two down!*

IS Chip Hilton's ankle all right?

Chip folded the paper carefully and placed it in his backpack. Biggie and Speed finished reading at the same time, and the three friends walked silently to the locker room. Neither Biggie nor Speed mentioned the "Batting Cage," but Chip knew they had read the article carefully.

Biggie's jaw was set grimly, and Speed's silence was entirely opposite his usual talkative disposition. The three boys had been friends a long time. Their silence right now said more than any words could express.

They dressed quickly and quietly and started for the field. Chip had never felt quite so determined about a baseball game as this one. When he took his turn at batting practice, he concentrated on every pitch as though meeting that ball meant the game. When Chip did that, it was bad news for some pitcher. He had a deadly eye. He looked the pitches over and passed up the bad ones until the pitcher had to get the ball in there or give him a walk. Then Chip dug in for the fat pitch.

Rockwell followed his usual practice of warming up all his pitchers—both of them. Chip took Lefty's throws and Carey caught Trullo. Then, just before infield practice, Rockwell gathered the team around him and announced the lineup.

"Rodriguez, right; Morris, short; Williams, left; Cohen, first; Hilton, catch; Schwartz, center; Collins, second; Badger, third; and Trullo, pitch.

"I've changed the batting order a bit. Maybe that'll help get us into the win column. All right, let's have a lot of pepper out there."

The stands buzzed when the crowd saw Trullo walk to the hill for his warm-up throws. Chip gave Nick a target. Trullo wound up and threw without any clue to Chip about his pitches. Pitchers usually employ several gestures to indicate what they are going to throw to the receiver when they are warming up. But not Trullo. He just blazed them in.

Chip walked out to the mound to check the signs with Trullo. Once again, Nick focused his eyes on the ground as he dug a little hole with the toeplate of his pitching shoe. Chip searched Trullo's face hopefully, but when he saw no sign of cooperation there, he pressed the issue a little further.

"I'm sorry about what I said last week in the game, Nick. Come on, let's work together and win this one. OK?"

But Trullo's attitude didn't change. He lifted his brown eyes and looked Chip up and down. One corner of his mouth lifted in a cynical smile. "You catch 'em, Hilton," he said. "I'll pitch 'em! Remember?"

Chip remembered. Without another word, he turned and took his position behind the plate. As he adjusted the mask on his face, he felt hopeless. Nick surely wasn't going to repeat last week's performance of pitching an entire game without signs, was he? He shook the thought off, suddenly feeling disgusted with his own weakness, and clamped his jaws tight. He'd give the signs, and Trullo could pitch 'em however he wanted. Chip Hilton would catch 'em either way.

The game was a nightmare. Trullo paid absolutely no attention to Chip's signs. But at least this time, he didn't even bother to pretend to shake them off. He took his time, used his lazy windup, and threw the ball where he pleased. Ironically, anyone watching the two players would have believed they were working in complete harmony.

Chip was having a difficult time. Speed's questioning gaze and the frequent huddles he was having with Chris Badger and Cody Collins indicated his bewilderment with the signs.

It was a tough game. Parkton was a strong-hitting club. Even Chip had to admire Trullo's pitching. Nick seemed to smell out each batter's weakness.

As the Big Reds came off the field for their turn at bat in the last of the third, Speed stopped Chip. "Look, Chip," he said, "I know Trullo isn't following the signs, so we're not following them in the field either. We're just taking a chance. But it's kinda tough and Rock's bound to get wise. We're all looking bad on the plays. Why don't you tell that fool off? If you don't do something about it, *I'm* going to."

"I'll handle it, Speed," Chip interrupted quietly. "It's my responsibility."

It was a close game all the way. O'Donnell, the Parkton pitcher, pitched to everyone but Chip and Biggie. Chip walked once and got a hit but was stranded both times. Biggie walked twice in a row. But O'Donnell pitched to the rest of the Big Reds. Only Red Schwartz was able to get a scratch single but, like Chip, was left on base.

When Chip was behind the plate, he stood in a semi-crouch. When he expected a curve, Trullo would drive the batter back with a high, fast one. With men on first and a sure steal coming up, Chip would get set for the fastball so he could move out a step and get a quick throw away, and Trullo would cross him up again by throwing a breaking ball low to the inside. Chip didn't even have a chance to throw to the base. He had several passed balls that he didn't have a chance to get his glove on.

In the fourth inning, Parkton scored. Trullo walked the first batter, and the next man fouled out to Chip trying to advance the man on first. The runner was nervous, and Chip was sure he was going down. Hopefully, he gave the sign for a pitchout, but Trullo threw the worst possible pitch, an outside breaker, which Chip barely stopped. He didn't have a chance to throw. Again, Trullo paid no attention to Chip's sign for a throw to second. The runner took a big lead and was nearly to third when Chip got the ball. On the very next pitch, Trullo threw one in the dirt that got away to the screen, and the score was Parkton 1, Valley Falls 0.

Chip stopped giving the signs and trying to guess the pitch. He just waited, ready for anything. Repeated trips to the mound did no good. Once, when Parkton had men on second and third with two down, Nick deliberately threw a beanball that narrowly missed the batter's head. Then Nick struck him out with a low one, outside.

Chip waited for Trullo that time and walked beside him to the dugout. "You'd better be careful, Nick. Coach doesn't like beanball pitchers," he warned. But Trullo ignored Chip completely.

The score had not changed when Valley Falls came to bat in the bottom of the inning; the big end of the stick was up. Speed Morris led off and hit an inside pitch on the handle. The ball trickled along the third-base line, and the Parkton third baseman elected to let the ball roll into foul territory. But the spinning ball held its line, and the speedy shortstop was safe.

Ted Williams was in a hitting slump. He had gone hitless in the opening game and here, in his seventh official time at bat, was caught again on a change-up that he popped to the catcher. That meant one away, and Speed Morris was still perched on first base. Biggie was up, and Chip waited on deck, with Red Schwartz in the hole. O'Donnell called time, and the Parkton coach walked out on the field. Chip knew what that was all about. So did everyone else! The Valley Falls fans whooped it up.

"What's the matter, O'Donnell? Scared to pitch to him?"

"Here you go, Parkton! Better pass 'em both, O'Donnell!"

After the Parkton coach retired to the visitors' dugout, O'Donnell monotonously threw four wide balls to the catcher and Biggie walked, putting runners on first and second. The Parkton coach had decided to violate one of baseball's maxims: "Never put the winning run on base with an intentional pass!"

Chip adjusted his batting helmet, yanked at his waistband, knocked his bat against each shoe carefully, and stepped into the box. Behind him, on the bench, he could hear the team yelling:

"Come on, Chip, sew it up!"

"Get a piece of it, kid!"

"Put the wood to it!"

Chip's knees felt a little shaky, but the feeling passed after he had taken a called strike. The next pitch was around his knees but on the inside, and the count was one and one. Again, O'Donnell broke a curve around Chip's knees, and the count was two and one. The Parkton hurler remembered Chip's fourth-inning single and was trying to keep his pitches low. Chip didn't try to outguess O'Donnell. He waited and watched the ball, taking the pitches as they came.

With the count three and one, O'Donnell bent another one down around the knees, and again Chip let it go by. It was a called strike, and the count was three and two. The next pitch had to be near the plate.

Biggie was taking a big lead off first base, and Speed was kicking dirt and moving back and forth on the baseline between second and third, trying to distract O'Donnell. But O'Donnell was crafty. He took his stretch, lowered his two hands and the ball to his waist, and then suddenly pivoted and threw to first base. A chagrined Biggie Cohen was caught flat-footed, an easy pickoff. Soapy Smith screamed to Speed Morris, "Come on!" and Morris barely beat the intended double-play throw to third. Soapy wiped his brow and cast his eyes skyward. That was too close to suit Soapy. It was two down now, and the tying run was on third base. It was up to Chip.

Chip stepped out of the batter's box and yanked his helmet a little lower over his right eye. O'Donnell stretched and tried to cross Chip with a fast one, shoulder high. But Chip was standing upright, and the strategy was lost. He leveled off and met the ball squarely. He knew by the ring of the bat that he had connected hard, and as he dug for first, he lifted his eyes toward the ball heading for the right-field fence.

There was a tremendous roar from the stands, and Chip lifted his eyes again to see the Parkton right fielder standing beside the fence and watching the ball soar over the barrier and far out into the street. Chip relaxed and slowed his pace. He jogged around the base paths, carefully tagging each bag.

His heart was pounding, and he took several long breaths to ease the choked-up feeling that had gripped him at the plate. He felt good now. It was his first home run of the season. Maybe that would make up a little for his catching.

Soapy was waiting for Chip on the third-base line and trotted along beside him all the way to the plate. Little Paddy grabbed Chip by the hand and pumped it vigorously. "Atta boy, Chip!" he said seriously. "Atta boy!"

That put the Big Reds out in front 2-1. Rockwell was talking to Mike Rodriguez when Chip reached the dugout. He clapped Chip on the shoulder. "Good hit, Chip. Good hit!" Then he surprised him by adding, "You take Rodriguez's place in right field when you go out!" He turned to Carey. "Carl, you're playing for Mike! Behind the plate!"

O'Donnell struck Red Schwartz out, and the Big Reds trotted out on the field full of zest. It was a new ball game now!

Chip had never played in the field although, like most players, he had caught fly balls in practice. He felt awkward out there by the fence, as though he were clear out of the game. The Rock had finally made the move everyone expected. Well, he guessed he could take it. He could play "a little part," as Doc would say. He'd have to if he wanted to play ball for Valley Falls. Anyway, he'd put the team out in front with his home run.

Trullo and Carey worked beautifully together, and the signs began to come through. Cody Collins flashed them to Chip. This was something, Chip reflected. Just as soon as Carey got behind the plate, everything began to click.

But Chip was wrong. Everything didn't click. The seventh opened with the Big Reds still nursing the one-run lead. Trullo hit the first batter. The next hitter laid down a sacrifice bunt along the first-base line that should have been an easy out, but Nick and Carl played, "I've got it—no, you take it," and both runners were safe.

Parkton suddenly came alive. The next batter met one on the nose, and the ball sailed high in the air and toward Chip. His breath almost stopped. The ball got smaller and smaller and then seemed to twist from side to side as a high-kicked football does when it noses down. Chip shifted his eyes away from the ball for just a second and then flashed them back. The ball was coming straight down into his glove. He squeezed the ball desperately and then gunned it toward third base.

But the runner on second beat the throw. As soon as the ball left Chip's hand, the runner on first sped down to second. Now there were runners on second and third, and only one away.

Ted Williams called time and trotted in to join Rockwell, Carey, and Trullo on the mound. Chip walked in as far as second base and waited. He knew they were discussing an intentional pass to fill the bases so there would be a play at any base—maybe a double play.

Rockwell decided to walk the batter. Trullo pitched four straight balls to fill the bases and then really went to work. He struck out the next batter, making it two away, and then got two strikes on the next hitter. That brought cheers of relief from the Big Reds fans. Carl Carey was talking it up and working Nick just right, it seemed to Chip.

Then it happened! Trullo threw a sharp breaker; the batter checked his swing. The umpire called time and waved the batter to first base and the runner on third home.

Ted again called time and sprinted in toward the home-plate umpire. Rockwell got there first, however, demanding to know what the call was all about. He soon found out. Carl Carey had tipped the bat with his glove, interfering with the batter's swing!

"Is that right, Carl?" Rockwell snapped. "Did you touch his bat?"

Carey nodded his head. "But it was an accident, Coach!"

Rockwell turned without another word and huffed his way back to the dugout. The run counted, and the score was tied with the bases loaded. Before the side was retired, Parkton tallied twice more. The score: Parkton 4, Valley Falls 2. And that's the way it stayed.

CHAPTER 13

The Hill Code

AFTER CHURCH, Chip carried the Sunday papers into the family room and placed them in his mother's lap. "Not so good, Mom," he said wistfully. "Same old stuff! 'Chip Hilton's days behind the bat are over!' 'Rockwell has finally tumbled to the fact young Hilton has lost his peg to the bases!' 'Rockwell waited too long to use Carey behind the plate!'" He dropped to a chair and studied his hands carefully.

Mary Hilton scrutinized her tall son thoughtfully. There was something more on Chip's mind than newspaper articles. At the breakfast table that morning, Chip had been far away, his thoughts focused on some personal problem. He had spoken only once or twice. She wished she could help, but Chip wasn't the kind of person who immediately confided his troubles. He tried to work them out himself first.

Chip wanted to think, and somehow it always seemed easiest to come up with solutions in the backyard. He took the bag of balls he had been accumulating, and soon the thud of hard-thrown baseballs echoed throughout the neighborhood. He wished Soapy would come over; he needed someone to cheer him up.

As if by magic, Soapy Smith appeared. He trotted around the house completely out of breath.

"Hi ya, Chip! Where's the glove?" he gasped. "Boy, I'm burning up! I need a workout!"

Without waiting for Chip's reply, Soapy bounded up the back-porch steps and rummaged in the corner behind Chip's practice bats. With a grunt of satisfaction, he pulled out Big Chip's old glove.

"Now," he said, "let's go to work! I got a feeling we're gonna be in there soon. Those two wise guys are gonna get bounced! Sure as today's Sunday. Beanballs, tipping bats, crossing up the guys—hah! Even the Rockhead'll catch on to that before long! And when he does, it'll be the grandstands for the Trullo-Carey combination!"

Soapy knew Chip Hilton just about as well as anyone could. This morning he had headed to Chip's early on purpose. Soapy had read the papers too. He didn't wait for Chip to answer but continued his one-way broadcast.

"All right, now, Chipper. Let's warm up nice and easy and then open up. OK? OK! Give it to me, right here, baby! Pretty soon I want to see that ole fireball! Right now, let me have that nothin' ball. Just a little ole easy pitch for control, kid. Loose as a goose, Chipper, that's the ticket. Now you're in the groove, big boy. Zip 'em in!"

After several thousand words, Soapy called time and let himself be invited to Sunday dinner. He wasn't too subtle about it. But then, Soapy was nothing if not faithful to his stomach. And he liked Mary Hilton's cooking. "It sends me!" he'd say, smacking his lips. "Inconceivably sends me!"

THE HILL CODE

Sunday dinners at the Hiltons' were something. Soapy didn't even mind helping wash the dishes afterward. He liked it because just about the time the dishes were finished, he could always rationalize the last piece of pie or cake and retire to the Hilton A. C., content to lie on the grass. Looking up through the tender, young leaves of the big maple tree, Soapy would dream away—dream about the day when the umpire would announce, "For Valley Falls: Hilton and Smith."

This afternoon, he had barely gotten comfortable under the tree when Speed, Biggie, and Ted Williams arrived. "Well," Speed said, "I see you've got yourself well-stuffed, again! Don't you have a home?"

Soapy rubbed his stomach and rolled his eyes. "Speed," he said, "I'll have you know when it comes to food I'm a pedicure!" He closed his eyes happily.

"Pedicure?" Speed roared. "You're that, all right! You sure are! You're *all* feet!"

Soapy turned imploringly to Williams. "Say it isn't true," he sang. "Say it isn't true."

Ted nodded. "It is," he said. "Wrong again, Soapy. You mean epicure. We have to get you a thesaurus for your birthday!"

"Thanks, Ted. A thesaurus! I just love books on dinosaurs!" Soapy smiled brightly, looking around the circle of friends.

In unison, the Hilton A. C. athletes held their noses and booed Soapy's latest witticism. But it kept the mood of a lazy Sunday afternoon.

The talk soon turned to the game. But Chip wasn't going to have any part of that. He was thinking about something else, something that had to do with the future, not the past.

STRIKE THREE!

"Here," Chip said, "you play catch with Soapy. I'm going to work."

"Wait," Biggie called, "we'll walk along with you."

Chip shook his head. "No, I'll see you down at the store later. Got an appointment!"

Chip struck out purposefully. He had reached a decision. This was going to be the showdown day. He wasn't looking for trouble with Trullo, but he felt going over to the Hill would make it clear to Nick that he was sincere and willing to go more than halfway to patch up their differences.

After Chip left, his four friends gathered in a huddle. Speed took the initiative just as he had Friday afternoon. "This has gone far enough," he said. "If you guys won't do something about it, I will!"

"I've been thinking about it, and I guess there's no time like the present," Williams said softly. "I'll go over right now! But no talking! You know how Chip is. He'll be ticked if he thinks we're butting in!"

Chip had been up on the Hill a lot of times. Before his high school days, he had played on the West Side Juniors and had visited the Hill for games in football and baseball against the South Side Hilltoppers. He knew he'd find Trullo up there today.

Trullo was there, all right. He and Carl Carey were playing in a baseball game. It was a beautiful day, and the Hill was crowded. Men, women, and a scattering of young kids were seated on the rocks and the side of the Hill watching the game. Over on one side, under some trees, a crowd of men in their early twenties were playing cards. Chip recognized Buck Adams, Peck Weaver, and Ken Carey in the group.

THE HILL CODE

Chip sat down to watch and wait. This was going to take longer than he had figured, but he was going to stick it out . . . get it over with once and for all.

When the game ended, Chip walked across the field to join Trullo and Carey. Trullo answered Chip's greeting rudely. "What are *you* doing over here?"

"Waiting to see you, Nick. I want to talk with you."

"Well, go ahead."

"Nick, I'd like to work out our differences. I'd like to know why you keep crossing me up in the games. It's not fair to the team, and I'd like to get it cleared up. That's why I'm here."

Chip paused, but if he expected Trullo to say anything he was disappointed. Nick merely grunted.

"I want to play on the team just as much as you do," Chip continued, "and when the coach tells me to catch, I'm going to do the best I can no matter who pitches. I try to do my best wherever the Rock uses me. But—and I'm saying it for the last time—the next time I'm catching and you cross me up, I'm going to call time and walk right over to the dugout and tell the coach the whole story."

For the first time, Trullo showed a spark of interest. "What'll you tell him?" he challenged.

"That you don't pay any attention to the signs!"

"What makes you think you're the only guy who knows what to pitch to a hitter?"

"I don't! But I'm supposed to flash the signs. You have the right to shake me off if you think I'm calling the wrong pitch."

Trullo's dark face was angry. "Well, aren't you big-hearted!" he said heatedly. His jaw tightened. "You run along, Hilton. Back to the West Side and the Sugar Bowl and to your hotshot buddies. Just remember one thing!

STRIKE THREE!

I'll pitch what I please whenever I pitch to you and you can snitch to the coach, the principal, and the school board for all I care!"

"What's doin' with you two?" Peck Weaver swaggered between the two boys. "Can't you guys hear?"

Trullo laughed. "Oh, this wise guy, here, came all the way over from the West Side to tell me how to pitch," he said. "And he's going to run to Rockwell if I don't pitch the ball just the way he wants it and where he wants it every time!"

"Is that right?" Weaver sneered. He brushed Trullo roughly aside and faced Chip. "You know what we do to snitchers over here on this side of the river?" he rasped. "No?" He took a step forward. "Well, I'll show you—"

Weaver struck out with his open hand. Chip evaded the slap and sidestepped quickly to the left. Weaver followed. This time his hand was clenched into a fist as he swung viciously at Chip's head. Again, Chip parried the blow and gave ground. Weaver was heavier and more powerful, but Chip was faster, taller, and in better condition.

Feelings of alarm and exultation suddenly gripped Chip. So this was what it had all been building up to: this was his chance to prove to Trullo, Carey, and everybody else that just because he kept going more than halfway, he wasn't afraid to defend himself. Just because he had a warm disposition and tried to be fair didn't mean he couldn't stand up for himself.

As Chip circled a little to Weaver's right and deflected another wild swing, he caught sight of the circle of faces that had suddenly ringed him and his antagonist. Trullo and Carey were grinning and watching every move intently. They were happy to see Chip in trouble. Behind those two, Chip caught a glimpse of the anxious faces of Chris Badger and Cody Collins.

Weaver was rushing wildly, trying to close in. But Chip was too smart to risk that. He gave ground, sidestepped quickly, danced to the left, back to the right, and gave ground again. He hadn't struck a blow.

Weaver rushed him again, both arms flailing. This time, Chip gave way about half a step. As Weaver's left grazed his chin, Chip struck out with all his strength at the sneering face. A beautiful right cross caught Weaver off balance and staggered him. His momentum carried him to one knee, but he was right back on his feet, choking and spitting as he came at Chip again.

Weaver liked a rough-and-tumble fight. But too many cigarettes and night after night of drinking hadn't equipped him for a fight in which footwork and boxing know-how counted. His breath was coming in tortured gasps, and he mouthed profanely as he tried to close in once more. Chip jabbed a hard left to Weaver's mouth, shuffled a half step to his right, and then put everything he had into a blow under Weaver's mauling left hand and straight for Peck's stomach.

Peck gasped in shocked surprise and half-fell forward against Chip's shoulder. The opening was perfect. Chip came across with a short left hook that landed high on Weaver's cheekbone and knocked the burly man to his knees.

Chip stepped back and dropped his arms, thinking it was over. A vicious shove from behind drove him over the top of Weaver, and the two toppled to the ground. This was the kind of fighting Weaver liked, but he wasn't ready for the opportunity, and Chip pushed him away and scrambled to his feet. Again, someone shoved him, this time away from Weaver. It was Ken Carey who faced Chip now. "That's enough, Hilton," Carey said. "Cut it out!"

STRIKE THREE!

Behind Carey, Chris Badger and Cody Collins tried to stop Weaver as he sprang to his feet, insanely angry. "Get out of my way," he bellowed, "I'll—"

"No, you won't, Peck!" There was a sharp edge to Carey's voice; a sudden strength empowered him as he faced the infuriated man.

Weaver looked at Ken uncertainly and tried to get around him, but Carey deliberately blocked him. "No, you don't, Peck," he said quietly.

Weaver focused his attention on Carey. "What's eatin' you?" he grated.

"Nothing! Except that I'm not going to let you beat up a kid, and I'm *not* going to see him ganged up on either."

Adams grasped Weaver by the arm and forced him back through the crowd. A short distance away from the crowd, he began whispering and explaining something that seemed to quiet his angry friend.

For a second time in less than a year, Chip trudged back from the South Side, unsuccessful in his attempts to bridge the gap between the two factions. The South and West Sides seemed further apart than ever. The feeling between the two groups was as deep as Valley River.

CHAPTER 14

Too High Up!

COACH HENRY ROCKWELL spent Sunday afternoon on the deck reviewing Friday's game and wondering why the Big Reds weren't clicking.

Late in the afternoon, Ted Williams visited and told him about the trouble between Chip and Trullo. "So that's it," he mused. "How could I have missed that?

"Are you sure about the signs, Ted?" Rockwell pressed. "Maybe you're mistaken?"

"No, Coach, I'm not mistaken," Williams said firmly. "Remember, Chip caught a *real* pitcher last year. Tim had more stuff than Nick will ever have! Chip never had a passed ball all season. And not many stolen bases either! No, sir! Trullo doesn't pay any attention to Chip's signs!"

After Williams left, Rockwell spent another hour in reflection. Williams, too, had mentioned Chip's pitching practice. But that wasn't important right now. The pitching could wait until Carey or someone else proved he could do a better job behind the plate than Chip Hilton.

What could he do about Trullo? He couldn't drop the kid just because he had been quarreling with Chip Hilton. He couldn't take sides.

Rockwell suddenly sat up straight and slapped a heavy hand across his thigh. "That's it!" he said. "That's it. I'll give the signs from the bench!"

On Monday, Ted Williams waited for Chip after lunch and got right to the point. "I saw the coach yesterday, Chip. And I told him all about the signs."

"What did you do that for, Ted?" Chip asked. "Everything would have worked out all right. Now, Nick will think for sure I told the coach because I was fed up about yesterday!"

"Frankly, I don't care what he thinks," Ted said. "It's part of my job as captain to tell the coach about things that hurt the team. The team comes first with me!"

Chip nodded his head. "Yes, I know, Ted. I'm sorry I said that."

Just before the end of Tuesday's practice, Rockwell informed the squad he'd arranged a practice game with Midwestern for Wednesday, and the squad would leave by bus promptly at 3:30.

"Coach Hoffman has invited us all to stay for dinner after the practice," he said.

The Big Reds always enjoyed the informal games with Midwestern, a private school located in Plains, a small community five miles from Valley Falls. Although Plains was nothing more than a crossroads town, the school was one of the finest in the country.

To be invited for dinner at Midwestern was something too. The Big Reds—particularly Soapy—always enjoyed that. The Midwestern boys dressed up for their meals, and Rockwell advised everyone that jackets and ties were a must. Rockwell cared about the way his athletes looked and acted off the field just as much as he was critical of their game uniforms and performance on the field. And, as much as the teenagers groaned, he knew they felt good when they looked good.

"Fawncy that!" Red Schwartz murmured. "We don't have to wear evening clothes! And I bought a copy of *GQ* for the occasion for nothin'! What's come over the little preppies!"

Soapy held up both hands and regarded his nails ruefully. "Oh, no," he wailed, "that means I'll have to have a manicure again tomorrow."

"Again!" Speed mimicked. "You've never had a manicure in your life!"

"I can dream, can't I?" Soapy retorted.

The next afternoon the team assembled at the foot of the long steps leading to the gym. Rockwell looked around the circle of eager faces, and the lines of his face softened. The Rock was pleased. Anyone would have been proud of these athletes. Every player was neatly dressed, and each possessed that rugged outdoor cleanliness of the healthy, well-conditioned athlete.

When the bus arrived, the boys piled in happily. The short trip to Plains was over almost before they had settled into their favorite seats, and the athletes hurried to the visitors' locker room to change into their uniforms.

After batting and fielding practice, Rockwell gathered the Big Reds before the dugout. "Now remember, boys, we're over here for a practice game and nothing more. We'll play this just as though it was an important league game, but there'll be no nonsense and no trouble.

STRIKE THREE!

"Today I'm going to shift the team around a bit and try to get a look at some of you guys who have been sitting in the dugout. I'll try something new with the signs too. I'll give all signs from the dugout to Coach Stewart and Coach Thomas who will be in the coaching boxes. They'll flash them to the catcher; he'll pass them along to the pitcher and the fielders. There'll be no shake-offs! Understand?"

The Big Reds looked at him in silence. Rockwell glanced from Trullo to Chip and then back to Trullo. "No shake-offs," he repeated, "and no changes! All right, we'll start in the field with the same lineup we started Friday except for you, Smith. You take Rodriguez's place in right field. Hilton, catching; Peters, pitching."

The Big Reds, first at bat, were set down one-two-three. Coach Hoffman had started Whitey Clark, Midwestern's veteran lefty and one of the best high school pitchers in the country. At the end of three innings, neither team had scored. It was an airtight defensive game.

When the Big Reds came in for their turn at bat at the top of the fourth, Rockwell surprised everyone by telling Carey and Chip to warm up. "I'm going to try you on the mound for a couple of innings, Chip," he said. "We could use a right-hand pitcher with a fast one."

Again, the Big Reds failed to score. Chip walked to the mound. When he toed the pitching rubber, he felt something was wrong. After his first warm-up pitch, he *knew* something was wrong. It was the elevation of the mound. All his practicing had been in the backyard, and he had forgotten to elevate the pitching rubber to the regulation twelve-inch height! He felt as if he were standing high on the back porch, throwing the ball down to Carey by the backyard fence.

TOO HIGH UP!

Chip increased the speed of his practice throws until he felt right and then stepped back off the mound and waited for the batter to take his place at the plate. The Midwesterners began to ride Chip. They knew he had never pitched before. Carey's pep calls contained a bit of sarcasm too. But Chip was an experienced athlete; razzing meant nothing. He was completely absorbed in making good as a pitcher. He was worried only about the mound and the necessary change in the angle of his pitching.

He walked the first man and then the second. His palms were damp and his heart was pounding. What a start! Speed trotted up beside him. "Come on, Chip. You can do it! Blaze 'em in! We'll back you up!"

Biggie, Cody, and Chris came trotting into the little circle too. Carey almost reluctantly joined them after calling time.

"They're waiting you out, Chipper," Biggie said.

"Just throw that fastball in there and let 'em hit, Chip," added Badger.

Chip was angry with himself. Of course Midwestern was waiting him out. The first two batters hadn't swung at a single pitch. Well, he'd throw straight over the plate and put all he had into the throws.

"Give me a target, Carl," he said. "I'm going to try to get the ball over. If they hit, all right!"

"Atta baby," chirped Cody. "Make 'em hit!"

But Midwestern didn't have to hit. Chip walked the next two batters and forced in a run. Bases loaded and none out. Carey gave him no target; he simply gave the signs he got from Stewart or Thomas. He seemed to gloat over each walk, and an ugly smirk of satisfaction high-lighted his face as he pegged the ball back to Chip.

In the field it was different. The whole infield was pepping it up, and booming in from the outfield, he could hear Ted, Red, and Soapy's shouts of encouragement. But it was no use; he couldn't get used to the mound. That thought burned him most of all. In his mind the word *alibi* kept repeating itself. Well, he'd keep it to himself.

He managed to get two called strikes across the plate but then threw three straight balls. Rockwell called time and walked out to the mound. "Guess this isn't your day, Chip," he said understandingly. "Forget it!" He waved to Trullo, who had been warming up with Mike Rodriguez behind the dugout.

Chip trudged back to the dugout. He was glad to bury himself under its shelter. He was bitterly disappointed at his miserable showing.

"Don't mind that, Chip," Stewart said kindly. "There're days when the best pitcher going can't find the plate!"

Trullo pitched well for the rest of the inning and for the remainder of the seven-inning practice game. Carey's catching was excellent. It was a pitcher's battle and ended with Midwestern on the long end of the score, 2-1. Although it was just a practice game and meant nothing in the records, the Big Reds took the defeat hard. It was always tough to lose to Midwestern.

CHAPTER 15

Mix up the Bats

THE HILTON A. C. was the busiest spot in Chip's neighborhood. After he had elevated the mound to the correct height, Chip worked a half hour every evening with Soapy catching. Speed moved to Chip's right as near as possible to the shortstop's position and Biggie took a position to Chip's left. Then they worked with Soapy on the signs.

Chip felt more confident after the Friday evening workout. Still, there wasn't much of a chance of Rockwell's using him in a regular game after his miserable performance at Midwestern, but he was going to follow Biggie's advice and be ready.

Saturday morning, the trip to Southern was a quiet one. The players had begun to worry about the season and their standing in the section. Soapy Smith tried once or twice to stir up some fun with his outrageous wisecracks, but his teammates were unresponsive. The Big

STRIKE THREE!

Reds were not facing this first game away from home with confidence. Their coaches had little to say even among themselves. When one of the bus tires blew at the outskirts of town, Chet Stewart muttered, "I hope that's not an omen!"

Chip felt uneasy as he warmed up Lefty for the game. He had a bad feeling about something—something that was going to hurt.

It hurt, all right! For the first time in three years of baseball, Chip Hilton sat on the bench! Rockwell named Trullo and Carey as the starting battery. Chip tried his best to act unconcerned, but it was no good. The sportswriters had been right. Chip guessed that even Nick Trullo had been right . . . but not about the snitching.

The Southern kids were good! They hustled every minute. The big, skinny pitcher who had been warming up had seemed too frail to have much on the ball. But you can't go by looks in sports. The boy proved that by striking out Rodriguez, Collins, and Morris, one-two-three.

Trullo and Carey got off to a bad start. A walk, a bunt that Trullo fielded too late, and a beautiful hit-and-run play filled the bases with none away. Southern was playing the Big Reds close, working for one run at a time.

The next batter bunted too. Carey and Trullo both chased the ball, leaving the plate uncovered, and the runner from third scored. The batter beat out the throw to first by a step.

Rockwell called time and strode out to the mound for a conference with Trullo and Carey. The deep-set frown lines between his brows moved precariously closer, and his thin lips were stretched in a straight line when he returned to the dugout.

Chip dug his nails into the bench in the dugout and watched Trullo and Carey. He was conscious of

Rockwell's worried glance but kept his eyes focused on the field. It was a tough spot for a pitcher.

Before the inning was over, Southern tallied four runs. At the end of the fifth, the score was Southern 4, Valley Falls 0. Trullo was in trouble all the way, but the Big Reds gave him wonderful support. Two blistering double plays by Speed and Cody saved him in the second and fourth innings.

When the Big Reds came in to bat at the top of sixth, Cohen was up. Biggie was disgusted; he hadn't touched the ball in his first two times at bat. But neither had anyone else.

"He's good!" Biggie muttered to Schwartz, about the Southern pitcher. "Where'd *he* come from? Where was he last year?"

Red shook his head. "I never saw him before!"

"Saw him before!" Ted Williams grunted. "I haven't seen him yet!"

Soapy wasn't giving up though. He bounded out of the dugout and began kicking bats in every direction. Little Paddy was horrified. He grabbed Soapy by the waist and began tugging for all he was worth.

"Cut that out! What's the matter with you?" he cried.

Soapy tried to explain that you were supposed to "mix up the bats" when your team couldn't hit. But Paddy wasn't going to fall for that!

"Nothing doing!" he cried.

Mixing up the bats during a hitting slump is an old baseball remedy. Sometimes it works. But not this time. Soapy had wasted his time, for Cohen, Schwartz, and Badger went down before the skinny Southern youngster as if they were hypnotized.

In Southern's half of the same inning, Trullo got into trouble again. He walked the first hitter. The next man bunted down the first-base line. Biggie charged in for the ball and tried for the out at second base. The runner was fast, had a good lead, and beat the throw. Speed winged the ball right back to Cody Collins covering first, but the throw was too late and both men were safe.

Chip watched Trullo closely. He had studied Nick a lot during the past six weeks; he knew the limits of the big player's temper. Nick's brown eyes were glittering now, and his dark face was clouded with anger.

Biggie took the short throw from Collins and walked over to the mound tossing the ball to Trullo.

"Too bad, Nick," Biggie said. "We let you down on that one. But stay in there. We'll get some runs for you yet!"

Trullo kicked a tuft of grass in disgust. "Yeah?" he growled. "How? You guys couldn't hit a ball the size of your heads!"

He turned away from Cohen and walked behind the mound. He wasn't even watching the runner on second. When the alert, heads-up base runner noticed Trullo was asleep, he dashed for third. Trullo heard his teammates' warning too late, but he threw the ball clear over Badger's outstretched arms and up against the low fence behind third base. The opportunist on third promptly raced home. The runner from second held up on third only because Ted Williams had seen the play coming and had backed up the throw.

The Southern fans and players really got on Trullo then. They jeered and dissed him with some good-humored razzing. The batter tapped the plate with his bat. "Come on, big guy," he bantered, "give me one I can hit!"

Trullo couldn't take it. His face was contorted with embarrassment and anger as he wound up and fired the ball right at the batter's head. The surprised boy didn't have a chance to duck before the speeding ball struck him right in the middle of the forehead. The boy stood perfectly still a moment, in shock, before he staggered and crumpled slowly to the ground. Players and coaches from both teams rushed to the plate. After a few minutes, the trainers carried the injured boy over beside Southern's dugout.

An angry murmur began to rumble through the stands. Rockwell countered the reaction by hustling Trullo into the dugout. On the way, he motioned to Peters to warm up. "You take Carey's place, Chip," he said quietly. Then he turned to Trullo, his black eyes searching the surly boy's face.

"Was that deliberate, Trullo?" he asked.

Trullo shifted his glance to the floor of the dugout. He shook his head slowly. "No, Coach," he said hesitantly. "I didn't mean to do it."

Rockwell studied the closemouthed boy carefully. Then he left the dugout and walked to the Southern bench. The injured batter was sitting up by the dugout, protesting that he was all right. The school doctor shook her head firmly, and the stands quieted as the injured boy was escorted from the field for observation at the local hospital.

The Southern fans had noted Trullo's discomfort at their good-natured razzing; they'd laughed at the big pitcher's obvious displeasure. They had naturally attributed his attitude to a temporary case of jitters because the breaks of the game had gone against him.

Now, they were not so sure the throw had been unintentional, not so sure the throw had not been an angry attempt to bean an opponent in a fit of temper. But they knew Rockwell was a coach who didn't approve of dirty play in any sport. His anxiety was obvious to everyone as he paced worriedly in front of the dugout, scarcely watching the game.

STRIKE THREE!

Chip knew there was something wrong with Peters as soon as Lefty threw his first warm-up pitch. The little athlete was pale and lacked his customary zest and nervous energy. Chip walked to the mound. "You all right, Lefty?"

"Sure," assured Lefty, "just got a little pain in my side—that's all!"

It might have been just a little pain in the side to Lefty, but his pitching quickly became a major headache to all the Big Reds. The ball had been automatically dead when the batter was hit, and the runner was still on third. A pinch runner had gone down to first for the batter Trullo had hit with the pitched ball. Lefty promptly filled the bases by walking the first batter he faced.

Chip called time and walked to the mound. Lefty's face was white; his shoulders hunched forward in a half crouch, and his stomach was drawn in. But there was a smile on the little hurler's lips.

"I'm all right, Chipper. It'll go away."

Chip turned and motioned toward the dugout. Rockwell walked quickly to the hill. "What's the trouble?" he asked. Before the question could be answered, he noted Lefty's face. "Hey, you're sick!"

Despite Lefty's protests, Rockwell led him to the dugout and called the Southern physician. The doctor quickly saw that she had two patients on her hands.

"This boy has a bad attack of indigestion, or his appendix is acting up. I'll take him right up to the hospital with our player," she said.

Rockwell sent Chet Stewart along with Peters and waved the Big Reds back on the field. Then he held a short consultation with the umpire.

Chip was standing by the plate, mask in hand, and overheard the conversation.

"The boy bad, Rock?"

"Looks like it, Lou. Kinda puts me in a hole. I haven't any pitchers left."

Chip's heart thumped. Without thinking he blurted out, "I can pitch, Coach—"

Rockwell shook his head. "We haven't anyone else left to catch, Chip. I can't put Carey back in the game—"

"Soapy can catch, Coach!"

"Smith? Why, he's an outfielder! He's never caught a game in his life!"

"I know, Coach, but we've been practicing every night."

Chip caught Rockwell's indecisiveness and unsnapped the chest protector and knelt to take off the shin guards.

"Soapy can do it, Coach. You'll see!"

Rockwell smiled grimly. "What have we got to lose?" he muttered. "All right, Chip. Warm up!" He turned to the dugout. "Smith!" he called.

Soapy eagerly broke from the group in front of the bat rack. "Yes, sir!" he panted. "Yes, sir! I'm ready, Coach!"

CHAPTER 16

What an Inning!

CHIP'S HEART was thumping as loudly as Soapy's fist making contact with his catcher's glove. Before he realized it, he had taken his warm-up pitches and Soapy, Biggie, Speed, Cody, and Chris were standing around him in front of the mound.

Soapy was pounding the glove with fierce determination. "We'll kill 'em," he declared. "Kill 'em dead!"

"This is it, Chip," Speed whispered. "Fire 'em in!"

"That's it," Biggie added. "Just throw them over. We'll back you up!"

"Yeah," Soapy urged, "just aim 'em for my big mouth!" He turned to Biggie and pulled the mask down over his face. "I think I look better this way! What d'ya think? But how will all the fans recognize me?"

As Chip's teammates trotted back to their positions, he suddenly felt a peculiar sense of loneliness. This was really strange. Here he was standing right in the middle of the diamond, surrounded by his friends and a couple hundred spectators, and he felt lonesome!

He took Soapy's sign and then realized the spot he was in—last of the sixth, bases loaded, none out, and the score 5-0 against him. The situation definitely didn't offer the most welcoming spot for a rookie pitcher! And he had wanted to pitch! Well, he'd asked for it!

He was jittery. His first two pitches were balls, and then Soapy walked halfway out to the mound and pointed dramatically at his mouth. Chip smiled. That did it; he loosened up and struck out the first batter. Then he felt better. The Southern crowd gradually forgot the earlier part of the game and began to yell for more runs. Chip worked the next hitter to a two-and-two count, then, fearing a walk, blazed one right across the middle. The batter met the ball a little late, but hard, and it sailed toward right field. It looked like a sure hit, and the runners all moved, but Biggie Cohen was in the right place. He leaped high in the air, caught the sharp line drive for the out, and slid into first base, beating the runner coming back to complete the double play. Chip shook his head and looked at Biggie thankfully. What a leap!

The Big Reds infield came running in, feeling as relieved as Chip.

"Whoa, I thought that inning would *never* end!" Speed said. "It must have lasted half an hour!"

Chip was up first at bat. He had replaced Carey, and Carl had been batting in the eighth spot. The tall Southern right-hander was tiring a little, but he could still fire them in. He was a little tight, though, because he had a no-hitter on the line. Chip spoiled that. He waited until the count was two and two and then blasted a triple between the right and center fielders!

STRIKE THREE!

The three-bagger must have upset the Southern hurler, for he walked Soapy, and the heavy end of the Big Reds batting order was up. Rockwell slapped Rodriguez on the back and talked quietly to him. The little leadoff hitter was grim-faced when he stepped up to the plate. He worked the count to two balls and no strikes. Chet Stewart, over in the first-base coaching box, gave him the sign for a take, and then another one. It worked. Both were balls, and Mike trotted down to first, loading the bases with none down.

Cody Collins was up. Cody was a stocky bundle of muscle, close to the ground and hard to pitch to. He had a good eye. With the count at two and two, he stepped into a curveball thrown low and golfed the ball over Chip's head just inside the left-field foul line.

Chip, Soapy, and Mike all moved with the hit. Chip came in hard, all set to hit the dirt, but it wasn't necessary. Speed was standing near the plate holding his bat at arm's length above his head—the sign to stay up. Soapy came tearing in, and Mike slid into third, barely beating the throw from the left-field corner. Cody took second.

Speed Morris was up next and doubled sharply to right center. Rodriguez and Collins scored on the hit. The tall pitcher had the usually reliable Williams handcuffed and struck him out. Biggie cracked the first pitch into the hole between the right and center fielders. Speed was off with the pitch and scored standing up. Biggie rested on second base. Then the Southern pitcher used eight pitches to strike out Red Schwartz and Chris Badger. That was all for the inning—but what an inning! The score: Southern 5, Valley Falls 5.

Chip was still on the mark. He allowed only one Southerner to reach first in the bottom of the seventh. The Big Reds were fighting desperately now. Chip had given them new hope. This game could still be won in extra innings.

The Big Reds had batted around in the top of the seventh, and Chip led off again in the eighth. He pulled the first pitch down the first-base line directly over the bag and stretched it into a double. Soapy struck out, Mike and Cody Collins walked, Speed popped out to the catcher, and Ted Williams struck out once more. Valley Falls stranded men on all the bases.

Southern managed to get two men on base in the bottom of the eighth, but Speed and Cody teamed up with Biggie again on another of their sizzling double plays to end the inning. Rockwell's long hours of practice with the keystone combination were paying off.

Cohen led off in the top of the ninth with the Big Reds still even. Biggie managed to reach first on a freak infield single when the ball hit his bat on the handle and squirmed along the third-base line slowly enough for him to beat out the third baseman's throw.

Then Schwartz, trying to advance Biggie with a bunt, cut under the ball and popped an easy out to the pitcher. Biggie barely got back to first. The winning run was on first, with one down. Biggie was slow, and Rockwell showed his confidence in Chip's ability to hit by calling for another bunt. Badger laid one down right in front of the plate and was an easy out at first. With Biggie in scoring position on second base, Chip came up.

Southern went into a conference on the mound. Chip stepped back out of the box. The Southern coach took a chance. He knew Chip was a dangerous hitter, and he decided to walk Chip to get at Soapy Smith for the third out.

Soapy's face was damp with perspiration, and everything about him expressed his determination to hit that ball. And hit it he did! The first pitch was a little on the outside for a ball. The second was a little high, but Soapy met it dead center with a powerful swing.

Biggie started with the crack of the bat. As Chip took off from first base, he followed the ball with his eyes just long enough to see it heading for deep left center. Chip was three long strides past second when Biggie turned third.

Chip knew that Biggie was in with the go-ahead run and watched Chet Stewart standing in the third-base coaching box. Then Stewart started running down the baseline toward home, and Chip knew he had to go all the way. He turned on the steam, and as he rounded third base, he heard Chet's warning shout.

"Slide, Chip! Slide!"

The Southern catcher was standing in front of the plate, poised to block him from the plate. This was going to be close.

Chip threw himself headlong at the plate behind the bunched figure just as the ball arrived. Chip and the catcher went rolling across the plate in a tangle of arms and legs, and Chip saw the ball spin out through the cloud of dust and come to rest just beyond the catcher's reach. He had made it! He was safe, and the Big Reds were out in front, 7-5!

Paddy Jackson and Mike Rodriguez pulled him to his feet, and as they celebrated toward the dugout, he saw Soapy perched on third. Soapy was patting himself on the chest and nodding his head toward the dugout and the stands on each side of the field. He was getting a hand too. He had delivered the goods!

Rockwell met Chip at the edge of the dugout. "Nice going, Chip," he said. Then as an afterthought, he glanced down at Chip's ankle and nodded toward it in a pleased manner. "Nice running too!"

WHAT AN INNING!

Mike Rodriguez tried hard to heed Soapy's pleading to "take the duck off the pond" but couldn't do more than trickle a slow roller to the Southern second baseman for an easy third out.

Chip took his warm-up throws and then toed rubber and looked down the alley at Soapy crouching beneath the batter. Three more outs and for the first time in his life, Chip Hilton would get credit for a victory as the winning pitcher.

He was shaky on the first pitch, and the unreal feeling he had experienced against Midwestern returned. He tried to concentrate on Soapy and "fire 'em in," but the more he tried, the more difficult it was to find the plate. He walked the first man and got himself in a hole with the second, trying too hard to hold the runner on first. Soapy tried to slow Chip down, but that was difficult to do. Chip was jittery. He walked the second batter to put men on first and second with none down. He was in hot water.

Soapy called time and walked out to the mound with the ball. The corners of the husky redhead's wide mouth turned up in a lazy grin, but his voice belied his easy bearing.

"Come on, Chip," he said. "We *gotta* win this one!"

Soapy took his time getting back to the plate, fingering a loose strap on his shin guards and finding something wrong with his chest protector, and then he couldn't seem to get the mask strap the way he wanted it. The umpire was impatient and pulled out his watch.

"Look here, young man," he said, "you're delaying the game! Do you want to finish this game or not?"

Soapy assured him that he wanted to finish the game as quickly as possible and managed to find the solution to his trouble without further delay. He crouched and gave the sign. Chip toed the rubber nervously and nodded his head. He blazed his screwball high and inside—too close.

Coach Del Bennett's words came back to him: "There comes a time, you know, Hilton, when the ball just has to be put over the plate!" He looked at the men on first and second. They were playing it safe, yet they were alert. They were watching out for a double-play ball.

Chip felt sure the batter was going to bunt. That was one of the reasons he was trying to keep his pitches high, avoiding a good ball. He took Soapy's signal and concentrated on the target. Soapy was pleading, "Stick it in here, Chipper! I'll take it, kid! Give, Chipper, give!"

Chip tried, but he couldn't find the corner, and it was ball two. Soapy again called time and walked out to the mound. He was wearing his best toothy grin.

"This guy's gonna hit a three-bagger!"

"Not unless I get it over!" Chip looked at Soapy sharply. "What do you mean by that?"

Soapy's smile was guileless. "He *said* he was!"

Then Chip got it. Soapy was pulling some of the stuff he himself had pulled many times when Tim Murphy got in a jam.

"You *would* joke at a time like this," he said wryly.

Chip took Soapy's sign for his curveball and hit the corner for a called strike. Soapy held the ball and turned to the umpire. There was a puzzled look on his face. "What's the count, sir?" he asked.

"You don't know?"

"No!"

The umpire looked at Soapy suspiciously and then growled, "Well, it's two and one!"

"Thank you, sir," Soapy said politely. Then he yelled to Chip, "It's two strikes and one ball, Chipper. Ya got him now!"

WHAT AN INNING!

The umpire tapped Soapy on the shoulder. "Pardon me, Mr. Smith, the count is *two balls* and one strike!"

"No?"

"Yes!"

The umpire called time. He raised his mask, and pushing his nose up against Soapy's mask, he yelled, "Now listen, Smithie, Smitty, Smoothie, or whatever your name is—quit stalling! Quit wasting time, or I'll forfeit this game to Southern! You understand?"

There was a hurt look in Soapy's eyes. He murmured meekly, "Yes, sir."

Chip's next pitch was wide of the plate, but before the umpire had time to call, "Ball," Soapy yowled and began hopping up and down, shaking his hand.

"My finger!" he hollered. "Time!" He turned to the umpire. "Time, please!" He shook his hand again. "Ow! Ow!"

"Time!" roared the umpire, glowering at Soapy. "And you'd better be hurt!"

Pop Brown came rushing out on the field with the medical kit. He grabbed Soapy's hand. "What's the matter? Your finger? Which one?"

Soapy dropped the catcher's glove and pointed to a wart on the back of his right thumb. "Hit me right there, Pop," he gasped. "Right there!"

Chip started for the plate, but Biggie stopped him. Biggie had yelled for the infield ball and began to play catch with Chip, knowing Soapy was pulling one of his acts. Biggie winked at Chip, jerked his head toward the plate, and tapped his forehead. Chip caught on and started throwing to Biggie, thankful for the opportunity to settle down.

A worried Rockwell joined the group at the plate. "What is it, Pop?" he asked.

STRIKE THREE!

Pop looked at Rockwell and slowly closed one eye. "Looks a lot like a wart to me, Coach," he said in a low voice, patiently rolling his eyes upward. "Mighty like a wart!"

Rockwell's sigh was a mixture of relief and resignation. "Think you can make it for the rest of the game?" he asked.

Soapy gave a speculative glance toward Chip, who was still playing catch with Biggie. He nodded his head. "Sure, Coach, I'll be all right! I'll walk it right off!"

"You sure will!" thundered the umpire. "And you'll walk right off the field and stay off if this game doesn't start in five seconds!"

The little rest was just what Chip needed. He felt at ease when play resumed and zipped his pitches right by the man at the plate and the next two batters to earn Valley Falls its first win of the season. Final score: Valley Falls 7, Southern 5.

As Chip walked toward the dugout, he breathed a deep sigh of satisfaction. His first win as a pitcher. He felt good!

CHAPTER 17

Nightmare Solitaire

COACH HENRY ROCKWELL hung up the phone, sat down in his soft leather chair and sighed. What next? It looked as though this season was completely jinxed. On his return from Southern, Doc Jones had called to tell him they had operated on Lefty Peters that morning for appendicitis. The little fighter was all right, but his baseball playing was finished for at least two months. At the beginning of the season, Rockwell's pitching staff had been weak; now he'd be lucky if he had a pitching staff at all.

Rockwell glanced at the clock. It was 3:15. He leaned back in his chair, thinking about Nick Trullo and Chip Hilton. He had asked Pop Brown to send the two boys to his office as soon as they appeared for practice. Now he really needed pitchers—and catchers too—unless Carey or Smith could take Hilton's place. Neither boy had proved himself yet, but that wasn't either's fault; Rockwell hadn't used them much. Now he'd have to use them.

STRIKE THREE!

Whenever Rockwell was worried about one of his teams, he played a little game with himself—a game he called "nightmare solitaire." Rockwell didn't use playing cards for his game. He used blank index cards. Today he was filling them in, one after the other, with various pitching combinations and batting orders. He was completely absorbed in his game when Nick Trullo knocked on the door.

The coach carefully studied the tall, sullen, and aloof athlete.

"I've been thinking about Saturday's game for the past two days, Trullo," he said thoughtfully, "and I'm still worried about that beanball. I'm not sure you were telling me the truth about that pitch.

"You've got the makings of a great pitcher, Nick. You have everything but control, and I mean mental control. I was watching you closely in the Southern game when the crowd was pouring it on you there in the last of the sixth. You lost your head completely! You told me the beanball was an accident. Thank heaven, the boy is all right.

"One thing is sure! If I thought for one second you tried to hit that batter, you'd never play any sport again at Valley Falls High School.

"One more thing! Something's been happening to the signs when you're pitching and Hilton's catching. I won't stand for that! I could give all the signs from the bench, but that takes a lot of initiative and judgment away from the players. I don't intend to give the signs from the bench anymore this season, but I do intend to see that every player observes and respects those used on the field! Understand?"

Rockwell waited expectantly, but Trullo said nothing. After a short silence, Rockwell excused him. "All right, Nick," he said kindly, "that's all."

NIGHTMARE SOLITAIRE

A little later, Chip Hilton sat in the same chair and faced Rockwell. Henry Rockwell never did things by halves; he never put off important matters once he was sure of his position.

"Chip, I just talked to Nick Trullo. I realize you two are not on friendly terms. There's something personal behind your attitude toward each other on and off the field. I wish I could work out your differences, but I guess you'll have to do that yourself."

Rockwell paused. Despite himself, he couldn't help comparing Chip's attitude with Trullo's. Chip had always been cooperative; he always gave everything he had in every game. Rockwell had heard about what happened on the South Side. For a moment, he was tempted to ask Chip what it was all about, but he changed his mind. He'd probably find out in due time. It had taken a lot of courage for this young man to go over there, let alone stand up to Peck Weaver in a fight.

"Now, Chip, you had your first taste of pitching Saturday, and you looked pretty good. So did Smith. I'll have to turn him over to Coach Thomas and see that he learns a little more about the art of catching. But we're here to talk about Chip Hilton. As I started to say before, I don't know whether you can pitch or not, but here's something you might be thinking about.

"Lefty Peters had an appendix operation this morning. He's through for a couple of months. That means the season." Rockwell waited for this to sink in and then continued, "And here's something else to think about!" He handed Chip a small card. Chip ran his eye down the list of names.

Collins	4
Morris	6
Schwartz	8

STRIKE THREE!

Cohen	3
Williams	7
Smith	9
Badger	5
Carey	2
Hilton	1

Chip read the names slowly and noted the positions carefully. Soapy was getting a chance in right field in place of Mike Rodriguez. Guess the Rock wanted to see if Soapy could keep on hitting.

Then Chip came to the last name. Hilton, number one! Was the coach kidding him? He flashed a glance up and across the desk. Rockwell was dead serious. That meant Chip Hilton was going to start on the mound against Seaburg. The Rock was really going to give him a chance as a pitcher.

He glanced down at the card again, studying Soapy's position in the batting order and the number that followed his name.

"What do you think about it, Chip?"

Chip swallowed. Now was the time. This was his chance to tell the Rock about Soapy.

"Why, Coach—er—I wish you'd give Soapy a chance to work with me. We've been practicing a lot together, and he's a good catcher, Coach. He's better than I am." Chip watched Rockwell hopefully.

Rockwell smiled. "He did a good job in that inning when you were a little up in the air, Chip, but we mustn't forget Carey deserves a chance to see what he can do too. You run along now and be ready for Seaburg!"

Chip was walking on air after his conference with Coach Rockwell. Every evening he and Soapy worked in the backyard after regular practice. Bill Thomas had taken Soapy in hand, too, and had worked him hard all week.

Soapy pretended he disliked the attention. Showing off his reading of Harriet Beecher Stowe, Soapy called Thomas a Simon Legree, but deep inside he was as happy as he could be. His great dream was that he would be Chip's regular battery mate. Every night in his dreams he lived through games and plays in which he and Chip were the stars.

Chip's pitching form was improving every day. He had learned to shield the ball with his glove and his right leg as much as possible. And he practiced mentally as well as physically. When throwing his different pitches to Soapy, he would visualize either a right-handed or a left-handed hitter and then try to use the pitch he thought would be most effective. Against right-handed hitters, Chip practiced stepping almost toward third base before sidewinding the ball diagonally at the plate.

Against left-handed hitters, Chip specialized on what Big Chip had called an "inshoot" or a "fadeaway." Coach Del Bennett had called the pitch a screwball and, after watching Chip throw his "incurve" a few times, had advised him to use it chiefly against left-hand hitters and sparingly at that because it took a lot out of the arm. Chip could control this pitch as well as his curve. His fastball had a "hop" on it now, too, and occasionally his curve turned out to be a slider.

Friday came and, with it, the *Yellow Jacket*. Like the Sunday papers, the school sports page was filled with the Big Reds' initial victory of the season. Chip rapidly scanned the story and then shifted to the "Batting Cage."

STRIKE THREE!

THE BATTING CAGE

LEFTY PETERS is out for the season! That's right! Appendectomy! What is Rockwell going to do about the pitching situation now?

SOAPY SMITH mixed up the bats midway in the game! But it didn't mean a thing until Soapy got into the lineup! How can Rockwell keep a hitter like Smith on the bench?

ROCKWELL has developed a great double-play combination in Speed Morris and Cody Collins! Why can't he teach his pitchers and catchers how to field their positions?

CHIP HILTON replaced Lefty Peters in the sixth inning with the bases loaded and was saved by a great double play by Biggie Cohen! Hilton's speed saved him again in the ninth! But a pitcher has to have more than a fastball!

NICK TRULLO has had poor support in every game he has pitched! Could that be because he's from the South Side?

Chip crumpled the paper angrily and started to throw it into the wastebasket. Then he reconsidered the idea and stopped. Instead, he smoothed out the paper and tucked it into his backpack. *Wait until the game this afternoon,* he thought. *You'll eat those words.*

CHAPTER 18

Starting Pitcher

CHIP STOOD in front of the dugout, smacking a closed right fist into his glove. This time he was going to find out whether Chip Hilton was a pitcher. The Rock was starting the lineup that had been on the card, giving him his chance as a starting pitcher.

A foghorn voice announced: "Batteries for today's game. For Seaburg, Thornton and Marlin. For Valley Falls, Hilton and Carey. P-L-A-Y B-A-L-L!"

The Big Reds dashed out on the field pepping it up, and seconds later Chip glanced around the infield, toed the rubber, and fingered the ball. He looked at Carey for the sign. Carl called for a curve. Chip shook him off, wound up, and blazed his fastball across the center of the plate for a called strike.

The leadoff man was short and crowded the plate. He was up there to get on base any way he could. Chip didn't want to lose him or get in trouble by giving him a base on

STRIKE THREE!

balls. He kept shaking Carey off each time and struck the batter out with three straight pitches, using nothing but his fastball.

When the ball came back around the horn, Chip motioned to Carey, and they met halfway up the alley. "I want to keep using the fastball, Carl," he said. "At least for an inning or so. OK?"

"Use what you want!" Carey grumbled. "I'm callin' what I think is right. I can't *make* you throw what I call for, you know."

Chip turned back to the mound more determined than ever to pitch a good game. He continued to shake away Carey's signs on each pitch until Carl got around to the fastball. He felt sure everyone in the stands was saying, "That Hilton wants to catch and pitch at the same time!" But the fastball worked. Chip struck out three men in a row.

In the second inning with two men away, the first on an easy grounder to Speed and the second by way of three strikes, Chip decided to try his curve. It worked easily and smoothly, and he had another strikeout. He smiled grimly to himself on the way to the dugout. If this kept up, he'd try his extra pitch—the blooper! But then he remembered that Carl didn't know about that one. Almost nobody knew.

He had been pitching to Taps Browning one evening in the backyard, and the ball had slipped out of his hand and looped up in the air. Somehow, it had come down across the plate.

Taps had laughed and said it was just like a jump shot in basketball. They had tried it again and again just for fun until Chip could control the pitch. He wanted to try it out in a game, but he wasn't going to risk using it until he was sure he was a pitcher. Then someone would be in for a surprise!

STARTING PITCHER

Chip's battle of wits with Carey was reaching a climax. Carey sullenly crouched behind the plate and gave the signals. When Chip shook him off, Carey deliberately turned his head toward the dugout, making it appear Chip was unwilling to cooperate.

Finally, Carey tried another method of showing his annoyance. He walked a short distance down the pitching alley each time he received the ball and then burned it back to Chip with all his strength. Chip caught it each time, but the sting of the ball began to hurt. A slow anger flushed Chip's face. He'd had enough of this.

The next time Carey burned it back to him, Chip walked right up to the plate. He placed his hands on his hips and looked Carey straight in the eye. "What's the matter with you?" he challenged. "What's the idea of burning the ball back every time?"

Chip neglected to call time, and the umpire ordered him to play ball. But Chip was too angry. The umpire took out his watch and began calling a ball against Chip every twenty seconds. Rockwell wasn't going to stand for that. He called time and hurried up to the two boys. "What's going on here? What's the trouble?" he demanded.

Carey replied angrily, "Hilton's trying to show me up. He won't follow my signs!"

Chip was just as angry. "That's not true!" he said. "I want to use my fastball! Carey wants me to use something else."

Rockwell settled the argument by ordering Carl Carey to the dugout and Chip out to right field to replace Soapy. Trullo came to the mound with Soapy behind the plate.

Chip ran out to his position in right field, thoroughly disgusted with himself. He could have kicked himself every step of the way. What had gotten into him? Couldn't he take it? Why make such a childish scene and involve Coach Rockwell? Even worse, he'd had a six-inning no-hitter going, and he'd thrown it away. Why couldn't he control the wild impulses that gripped him so often lately?

Chip Hilton wasn't the only player on the field who was feeling bitter. Nick Trullo was in no mood to pitch. He had watched Chip set the visitors down in regular order during six long innings, and he had hoped something would happen to spoil that no-hitter. Nothing had! To make things worse, Hilton seemed to have gotten the best of the argument with Carl Carey because Carl was benched and Hilton was still in the game!

Nick was completely consumed with jealous anger. He fired eight warm-up pitches back to Soapy without even thinking about control or the situation the team was in. He wanted to hurt someone, and Soapy seemed the most logical target for his anger. Smith and Hilton were pals. Why had Rockwell taken Carl out of the game instead of Hilton? Hilton always got the breaks with the coach. He always got special treatment from Rockwell. And Nick wasn't going to forget for a long time the lecture he'd taken in Rockwell's office. Hilton had snitched about the signs. That's why he's Rockwell's pet!

When Trullo threw his last warm-up pitch, Soapy fired a sizzling peg down to second that narrowly missed Trullo's head. Soapy had a strong arm. After the throw, Soapy walked out to the mound.

"You want the usual signs, Nick?" he asked.

"What do you think I want?" Trullo growled. "That is, if you know what they are."

"I know what they are, Nick," Soapy said confidently. "Don't forget the count is two balls and one strike. And there's one down with nobody on—"

"You think I'm blind?" Trullo snarled. "I can see there's nobody on base! Clown!"

Soapy's face turned scarlet, but he held himself in control.

"Look, Nick," Soapy said, "maybe I'm just a clown in your opinion, but when I'm playing on a team, I like to play to win. Let's work together like we ought to."

But Trullo ignored Soapy and turned away as if Soapy were nothing to him. Soapy walked slowly back to the plate. Out in right field, Chip watched the meeting in front of the mound and was wondering what had happened. He knew how much this chance meant to Soapy.

Chip leaned forward with his hands on his knees and concentrated on the game. A quietness gripped the Big Reds; there was no chatter, no life. Chip straightened up. This was no good!

"Let's go!" he bellowed. "Where's the old pep?"

Trullo pitched too fast. Soapy tried to slow him down, but Nick was impatient and fired the ball back to the plate almost as soon as he got it. He walked the first man. He walked the second.

The next batter laid down a perfect sacrifice bunt along the first-base line, and Trullo fielded it efficiently. There was no chance for a play at second, but Trullo's throw to first was too hard and too fast. The ball went through Cohen's glove and out to Chip who had come in to back up the play. The runners held up at second and third, and the bases were loaded with one away.

Trullo was blazing mad now. He threw his glove down on the ground and stood glaring at Biggie Cohen. Chip had relayed the ball to Biggie, and now the big first baseman walked toward Trullo with the ball in his hand.

Trullo was muttering and glaring at Biggie with a rage-contorted face when Rockwell trotted out on the field and called time. He motioned to Soapy to join him with Trullo in front of the mound.

"Settle down, Nick," Rockwell said softly. "This game isn't lost! Don't get upset because of one little play." He placed a hand on Nick's arm and looked him directly in the eyes. "Remember what we were talking about the other day in my office? About control?" He paused for a second and shook Trullo's arm gently. "All right, then, get a grip on yourself!"

Trullo tried to cut the corners and to avoid giving the batter a good pitch, but this was costly. With the count at two and one, he hooked a spinning inside pitch that the umpire called a third ball. That was too much for Trullo. As Soapy fired the ball back to him, the hot-tempered hurler charged toward the umpire.

"What's the matter with you?" he yelled. "Can't you see anything except the middle of the plate?"

Trullo's face was convulsed with anger. He hurled his glove and the ball to the ground in a gesture of impotent rage. The ball rolled across the third-base line and back toward the grandstand with Soapy in quick pursuit. The runners began to move. Soapy chased the ball and pegged it to Biggie Cohen, who was covering the plate. But it was too late. Two Sea Bees scored, and the third runner danced in triumph on the bag at the hot corner.

Again, Rockwell called time and walked out to the mound. This time, his voice was sharp and his eyes were hard when he spoke to Trullo.

"Can't you control your temper, Nick? Don't you want to pitch for this team? Do you realize what an exhibition you're making of yourself?"

Rockwell took the ball from Biggie and placed it in Trullo's hand. His voice softened a bit as he continued, "You're the only pitcher left, unless I bring Chip back from right field. Come on, pull yourself together!" When Rockwell mentioned putting Chip back on the mound, Nick's blood boiled.

He walked to the mound and blazed a sharp curve that cut under the batter's feet. Soapy was able to stop the ball by making a dive. It was ball four, and the batter trotted down to first as Soapy scrambled after the ball and drove the third-base runner back with a fake throw. Soapy walked slowly out halfway to the mound, watching the runner on third. He stopped and beckoned to Trullo. Nick didn't move.

Soapy stood there indecisively for a second and then backed up to his position behind the plate. He crouched and flashed the sign. Trullo didn't even look for the sign or wait for Soapy to rise from his squat to a crouch. Nick just fired another curve at the batter, which broke down to Soapy's left just like the first one. This one got completely away, and the man on third scored while the runner on first sped all the way around to the hot corner.

Soapy recovered the ball and again faked toward third. Then he tossed the ball to Biggie in front of the plate and trotted directly out to the mound.

Rockwell was standing in front of the dugout, intently watching the proceedings. Soapy had followed Trullo clear to the back of the mound and was talking rapidly.

"Look, Nick," Soapy declared, "you crossed me on both those pitches! I'm not going to take it! You understand? You've been gettin' away with murder all season. You crossed Chip up time after time, and he kept it to himself and took a razzing from everyone! Even the Rock! But you've crossed me up the last time! Even if I *never* catch another game, I'm not going to take it!"

STRIKE THREE!

The ugly sneer on Trullo's lips, along with his sour expression, distorted his face. "What are you going to do about it?" he rasped.

"I'm gonna tell the coach!" Soapy retorted. "And right now!"

Soapy didn't have to tell the coach. Rockwell had again called time and quietly approached the two intent boys. He walked up on them unnoticed and heard the last part of their angry exchange.

"What's the trouble now?" he demanded.

Trullo lowered his eyes and said nothing. But not Soapy! Soapy spoke straight out without wavering his challenging stare.

"Nick crosses up the pitches! He doesn't shake 'em off or anything—just throws what he pleases!"

"Is that true, Nick?" Rockwell asked quietly.

Trullo said nothing. He stood there with a tense mouth and an angry scowl on his face.

"All right, Trullo," Rockwell said evenly. "Turn in your uniform!"

CHAPTER 19

Eating Their Words

SOAPY THUDDED the ball into the catcher's glove then handed it to Chip. "Man on third and one down, Chipper. One ball on the batter." He lowered his voice and continued, "This guy looks like a pushover—a sucker for a curve!"

Behind him, Chip could hear the team responding with its old spirit; the players were chanting just as they had in the first innings. He faced away from the plate and picked up the small rosin bag. Out in right field, Mike Rodriguez was back in his old position. Chip stepped up on the mound and took Soapy's sign.

His first pitch was a slider that nicked the corner for a called strike. Chip had stepped toward third on that one and twisted his pitch back toward the plate. The next one was a fastball with a hop for strike two. The batter swung late on that pitch and struck out on another curve. Soapy had been right. The batter was a sucker for a hook. That made it two away.

STRIKE THREE!

The next hitter got around slow on the very first pitch and fouled a high one to Biggie near the Seaburg dugout for the third out.

When the Big Reds came in for their half of that disastrous seventh inning, they were greeted by the stretch from the home fans. Most of the people in the grandstand remained standing. They seemed to feel now was the time!

The big end of the order was up, and Cody Collins came through with a sizzling single between the Seaburg shortstop and second baseman. Speed, up next, met one on the nose, which was too hot for the second baseman to handle. Cody went all the way to third on the hit-and-run play while Speed held up at first.

Red Schwartz followed, and on the first pitch—a called strike—Speed was off like lightning and slid safely into second base. The slide was unnecessary. The Sea Bees catcher didn't even risk the throw. Schwartz, determined and stubborn, fouled off three straight pitches and then struck out with a mighty swing. Biggie Cohen was up. He hadn't hit anything but his glove all day.

Little Paddy Jackson, who had arrived late from school and was still trying to get fully dressed, handed Biggie his favorite bat and gravely informed the big first baseman he was past due. "Way past due!" Paddy solemnly admonished.

Cohen caught up quickly. He met the second ball solidly. The Valley Falls fans went wild with excitement as the ball sailed lazily up, up, up and over the right-field fence. Cody and Speed scored as Biggie trotted slowly around the bases. On the mound, Thornton, the Seaburg pitcher who had almost had the game on ice, shook his head in bewilderment. Cohen's home run had tied the score: Valley Falls 3, Seaburg 3.

EATING THEIR WORDS

The game turned into a pitcher's battle from then on. It continued through nine innings and right up to the bottom of the eleventh. Seaburg hadn't collected a hit, and Valley Falls had been held to three singles and Cohen's home run. The three-all game was played tightly all the way.

Chip's control was perfect. Everything seemed to click. His fastball was hopping, his curve was sharp, and his screwball was bending as though he were pulling it with a string. He had pitched perfect ball for eleven innings. Seaburg had scored only on Trullo's walks and bad throws.

In the bottom of the eleventh, the Big Reds came up. Thornton was tired. He walked Speed, struck out Red Schwartz, and got Biggie on a foul tip to the catcher. Speed had stolen second on Red's third strike. He waited on second for Ted Williams to bring him in—or, as Soapy would say, to "take the duck off the pond."

Ted had been shackled by Thornton all afternoon, and again Speed was given the steal sign. Thornton concentrated on Williams for the third out, and on the first pitch Speed dashed to third. The catcher rifled the ball hurriedly, but the speedster had too big a lead and was too fast. He slid under the third baseman safely.

Thornton blazed a fast one around Williams's wrists, and the call was one and one. Speed stood listlessly on the bag during the pitch and on the catcher's return throw to the mound. In spite of his knowledge of Speed's base-running ability, Thornton fell for it. He merely glanced at the passive figure and then took a half windup.

Too late, he realized his mistake. The motionless figure on third exploded into action and dashed for the plate. Thornton's throw was hurried and high. Ted

STRIKE THREE!

Williams helped Speed by taking a full cut at the ball, hampering the catcher for a second.

Speed slid wildly across the plate with the winning run a split second before the catcher dropped on him with the ball. The game was over! And Chip Hilton had crashed the schoolboy "Hall of Fame" with a no-hitter!

That was about the happiest weekend Chip had enjoyed in months. The Saturday and Sunday papers gave him big coverage. Soapy was delirious with joy because of Chip's success and his own contribution behind the plate. Petey Jackson bragged at every opportunity about his ability to "pick a winner" and how he had old Leroy White on the run. Mary Hilton was thrilled by the accounts of her son's great pitching. John Schroeder and Doc Jones hung around the store both days, listening to every word about the game, and Chip's teammates were comparing him to the great Tim Murphy!

Only three people in town had forgotten the Seaburg game by Sunday afternoon. Coach Henry Rockwell, Chet Stewart, and Bill Thomas had smilingly accepted the congratulations of their Saturday golfing partners, but on Sunday they were sitting on Rockwell's deck up to their ears in a strategy session. They were worried about the nine remaining games, some of them only three days apart. And with only one *inexperienced* hurler!

"We've had nothing but bad news since the start of the season," Rockwell said gloomily. "About the only thing that's looked like good news is the way Chip pitched Friday and the way the club backed him up. But *one* pitcher can't do it!"

"And maybe Friday was just one of those things," Thomas offered anxiously. "Maybe Hilton's just a flash in the pan!"

"He's no flash in the pan, Bill," Stewart said. "He always comes through in a pinch. Chip's a clutch player!"

"I know, I know," Thomas amended hastily. "I meant as a pitcher!"

"Well, even if Hilton *does* turn out to be a pitcher," Rockwell interrupted, "he couldn't pitch all the games. They're too close together!"

"They're not too bad, Coach," Stewart interrupted hopefully. "Listen to this." He pulled the schedule card out of his pocket and slowly read the dates. "The 21st, 25th, 28th—all at least three days apart. And then in June, we play the 1st, 4th, 8th, 11th, 15th, and the 18th!"

"That isn't as bad as the schedule Tim Murphy carried last year," Thomas said.

"Perhaps not," Rockwell said slowly, "but Tim was a senior and an experienced pitcher. And don't forget we had Rick Hanson in the bullpen all year, and he relieved Murphy in plenty of those games. I don't like to use a young kid too often. Chip's never pitched before, and we could easily ruin his arm. I won't take a chance on that, even if we have to lose them all."

"But he's young, Rock, and he's got a strong arm."

"All the more reason to protect it," Rockwell said shortly. "No, we'll watch him closely and be sure he throws hard only every other day. Chet, you work out a schedule for him, and, Bill, you concentrate on Carey and Smith. I wish I could find out what's wrong with that Carey kid. Maybe now that Trullo's gone, he'll change his attitude!"

Sunday afternoon on the South Side Hill was not exactly a pleasant one for several people. Nick Trullo and Carl Carey were sitting disconsolately on the big rock watching the baseball game, and a little farther away, hanging apart from the crowd, Buck Adams and Peck Weaver were ruefully going over their bad luck.

"What got into Nick anyway?" Weaver complained. "We had it in the bag until he went haywire. Why'd he wanna do that? What did he hafta get bounced for?"

Buck Adams was the dominant figure and the brains in this partnership. His mind was working furiously. The psychology scheme hadn't worked out very well for the past two games. They had overplayed their hands somewhere along the line.

"We went too far," Adams murmured half aloud.

"What'd you say?"

"I was just figuring how we went wrong," Adams explained. "We prodded Nick and Carl a little too far. Especially Nick. We forgot about that lousy temper of his. Now we're going to have to play it smart if we're gonna break even—much less get ahead! We've got to make a killing along the line somewhere. I think we'd better lay off for a week or two and then pick a pot!"

"But how you gonna do it?" Weaver persisted. "That smart dodo of a Hilton looks like a better pitcher than Nick to me." He paused and rubbed his rough chin reflectively. "I shoulda polished that kid off that Sunday he was here. But good!"

Adams glanced at Weaver's right eye, which was still surrounded by a faint, bluish bruise. The side of Buck's mouth twisted into a slight smile, but he said nothing.

Peck pointed toward Carey and Trullo. "Carl there," he said, nodding his head in the boys' direction, "is gonna lose his catching job too. That crazy Smith is as good as he is, and, besides, Smith's tight with Hilton."

"Could be," Adams said thoughtfully. "But there's one thing for sure—Carl's gotta get back in the lineup. We can't do a thing without *him!*"

EATING THEIR WORDS

Weaver was still watching Trullo and Carey. "Wonder if there's any chance of Nick gettin' back on the team?"

Adams shook his head. "Doubt it. Carl said the coach told Nick he was through. To turn in his uniform. Rockwell's tough!"

"Yeah, but those coaches are all softies where kids are concerned. Bet he'd take Nick back if we—what'd you call it, Buck—psyched him, right?"

Adams smiled. "Could be, but I don't think Nick would go back if he could. He's plenty burned up with Rockwell and *all* the West Side crew!"

That afternoon, Rockwell talked to Chip for half an hour about pitching and impressed on Chip how important taking care of his arm was to the team and to his own athletic future. "You'll have to carry the whole pitching load, Chip. At least, until we can scout around and find someone to help out. It's a tough assignment."

"But, Coach, I've been throwing every day for the past six weeks! Hard too! My arm is strong. I won't get tired!"

"I hope not! But from now on—and this is an order—you're not to do any throwing except at regular practices."

Against Dulane, Chip pitched like a big leaguer. He limited the Northerners to four well-scattered hits for a 5-1 victory. He might have shut them out except for an infield error.

On Friday, Chip could hardly wait to get his copy of the *Yellow Jacket*. He was wondering what the "Batting Cage" editor was going to find wrong with the team—Rockwell or Chip Hilton this time. At noon, he hurried to the gym foyer and purchased his copy. He walked over to the baseball trophy case and opened the paper to the sports page.

STRIKE THREE!

THE BATTING CAGE

IS our face red! This sportswriter has been all wrong about one of the greatest athletes in Valley Falls history! Sure, you guessed it! CHIP HILTON! Apologies, Chip. Our error!

IN an earlier issue of this column, we stated that Nick Trullo, who shaped up as the best pitching prospect for this year's team, said he'd "pitch to Carl Carey or no one." Was that the reason he was asked to turn in his uniform? (Two men don't make a team!)

WE started this column with an apology so we might as well keep it up! Many regrets for overlooking the sterling play of Speed Morris and Biggie Cohen! Don't the Big Reds' opponents believe in nicknames?

AGAINST Seaburg, Speed Morris stole second, third, and then home to score the winning run in the bottom of the eleventh!

BIGGIE Cohen's big bat has batted many a big run across the plate for the Big Reds. Biggie stands for Mr. Big when it comes to batting!

CHAPTER 20

Repeat Performance

THESE WERE happy days for Chip Hilton. Sometimes he felt as if he were dreaming until he got out the scrapbook and read the enthusiastic accounts of the pitching feats of the "strikeout king." Best of all was the change in Carl Carey's attitude. Alternating with Soapy Smith as first-string catcher, he seemed to have completely gotten over his sulky lack of cooperation with his teammates. In the coaching box he was on his toes, and Chip felt he could finally depend on the little South-Sider's calls.

However, Speed and Biggie weren't so sure yet. The change was too sudden, and when Chip wasn't around or couldn't hear them, they suspiciously discussed Carl Carey's new turnaround.

But at last, the Big Reds were a fighting, hustling, cooperating team. Williams and Cohen had found their batting eyes, and Chip still was hitting well over the .500

mark. No longer was Valley Falls doubtful of the team's destination; it was headed for the state championship. Not cocky—just determined and sure.

Puzzled at first by Carey's positive change in behavior, Chip figured it was because of Trullo's absence, one of the Rock's heart-to-heart talks, or perhaps simply the thrill of winning games. But whatever the reason, the young catcher's about-face tremendously gratified the gray-eyed teenager, who had become the pitching champ of his father's long ago dreams.

And so as the mellow May days sped past, Valley Falls kept on winning, and Chip Hilton kept on pitching sensational ball. After the Dulane victory at home, the Big Reds took Salem away and three days later knocked off Delford at home. Then came three games during the first week in June, Coreyville and Stratford away and Dane at home, all chalked up in the victory column.

Even Coach Rockwell and his two assistants began to look with crossed fingers at the championship of Section Two as a neck-and-neck race between Valley Falls and its ancient rival, Steeltown—each with an 8-2 record.

Steeltown was, as its name implied, a steel mill town, and the men who turned out the pig iron and steel the town was famous for were strong and had been for generations. The population was primarily Polish, Lithuanian, Swedish, and Norwegian. The athletes who played on the high school teams were well named. The Iron Men, year in and year out, fielded outstanding teams in football, basketball, and baseball.

Every Valley Falls fan was talking now about the game with Steeltown at Valley Falls on Saturday, June 18. If the Big Reds could get by Delford again, only Steeltown would stand between Valley Falls and the championship of Section Two and maybe even of the state!

REPEAT PERFORMANCE

But Delford was not to be taken lightly in spite of the treatment the Big Reds had dished out two weeks earlier. Delford and Valley Falls were located only fifty miles apart and were bitter competitors in every sport. The second game was to be played at Delford. The competition was all the more intense because Coach Jinx Jenkins, Delford's veteran coach, and Hank Rockwell were bitter foes.

Saturday was a beautiful day for baseball—not too warm, not too cool. It seemed the road to Delford was a one-way traffic lane; every car in Valley Falls appeared headed to the game.

In the bus, despite Soapy's and Red Schwartz's hectic arguments, Chip thought back to the football game in Delford the previous fall. He had passed Delford to death to win a bitter, dog-eat-dog game by a score of 29-28.

The Big Reds were restless and anxious that afternoon both at bat and in the field. The Delford fans were quick to get on Chip's case, razzing, jeering, and heckling. But as inning after inning went by and Chip kept firing pitches and setting Delford down hitless and scoreless, their attitude changed. They began to pull with and for the tall, long-legged, determined kid. Chip was in the zone! Soapy didn't have to open his glove wide to get that "crack" he delighted to use.

The Delford fans knew this boy. They knew him well. They knew all about his football, basketball, and baseball skills. But now, they sensed they were witnessing something big, something important happening in the life of a high school pitcher. In spite of the bitter rivalry between the two schools and the two towns, they began to pull for him. To pull for a no-hitter! Even if it was against the home team! Against their own kids! Real athletes and real sports fans understand moments like this when

STRIKE THREE!

their admiration for spirited athleticism knows no sides and extends beyond the contest between two teams.

All of Jenkins's bellowing, tricks, and maneuvers meant nothing. Chip had Delford handcuffed. Chip didn't realize he was heading for his second no-hitter until the last of the fifth. But his teammates knew it. They had known it almost from the start, and they had gone out to get him some runs. They got him three, and that was enough! Chip kept the heat on, and then it was the last of the seventh, two down, and one batter to go for a no-hitter!

The count was two and two. Chip was holding a brand-new ball and remembering that other no-hit game ball resting in the baseball trophy case at Valley Falls.

Chip rubbed the stitches carefully and, in spite of himself, wondered if Valley Falls would get the ball even if he did retire this last hitter. He glanced over at Coach Jenkins in front of the Delford bench and then down the alley at Soapy. A perspiration-soaked mass of loyalty, Soapy had his jaw set as square as a block of concrete.

Chip wound up and blazed his screwball right at Soapy's glove. The hitter was late and low. His bat cut under the ball, and it went spinning crazily in the air high over the Big Reds bench. Soapy and Biggie tore after it. But Soapy got there first. He crashed into the wooden roof of the dugout, leaned far over, and caught the ball.

Everything went out of Chip then. He was completely oblivious to the cheers of his teammates and the Delford fans. He was dead tired. However, as he walked wearily toward the dugout, he saw Soapy race to the other side of the field and toss the game ball into the hands of Delford's Coach Jenkins. For a moment, he felt like going over and asking for the no-hit ball, but he changed his mind and continued to the dugout. There his cheering teammates and fans pounded him on the back, and the ball didn't matter.

But it mattered to the Big Reds. They confronted Soapy in front of the dugout.

"What did you do that for?"

"Man, it says in the rule book the winning team gets the game ball!"

"You crazy?"

Soapy remained calm. "Nope," he said haughtily, "I'm not crazy!" The familiar wide grin spread across his mischievous face. He tucked his hand behind his chest protector and brought out a shiny, new ball.

"Here y'are, Coach," he said proudly. *"This* is the game ball. The one I gave Jenkins was a practice ball. Ask Paddy!"

Paddy nodded vigorously. "Yep," he said, "yep, I gave Soapy an old ball!"

Soapy threw back his head and laughed with all his might. "Yep, Coach," he managed, "you can put that one alongside the state championship ball we're going to get June 25th."

CHAPTER 21

Integrity on the Hill

VALLEY FALLS was baseball crazy. Everyone was talking about the Big Reds and the section championship. In Steeltown, it was the same. All the Steeler fans felt their Iron Men were the best team in the state. The two teams were vying for the top spot in their section. It all pointed to a showdown on Saturday, June 18, when the two were scheduled to meet at Valley Falls.

The Big Reds had already won their way to this final game and were in a position to possibly back into the section championship if Steeltown lost to Weston on Wednesday. Edgemont, Section Three champion, was scheduled to play at Valley Falls on the same day. But the Edgemont game meant nothing in the Section Two standings.

Chip wanted to pitch against Edgemont to see if he could beat the champions of Section Three. Edgemont was already listed in the top half of the draw for the championship games at the university. But Rockwell had different ideas. He talked it over with Chet Stewart and Bill Thomas and decided to use Soapy Smith. Soapy was no pitcher, but he had a strong arm and excellent control. There wasn't much choice for the harried coaching staff.

The stands were filled with cheering fans Wednesday afternoon. A happy, enthusiastic crowd razzed the umpire when he walked out in front of the grandstand. But a groan went up when the batteries were announced.

"For Edgemont, Green and Benson. For Valley Falls, Smith and Carey." P-L-A-Y B-A-L-L!

Soapy wasn't so bad! He simply wound up and let 'em fly. It was effective. His pitches worked chiefly because the Big Reds gave him airtight support. In the seventh inning with the score tied at three, Soapy got into trouble and the bases were loaded with one down. Rockwell listened to Chip's pleas then and sent him in for Mike Rodriguez. Carey went to right field, and Soapy went behind the plate. Rockwell had decided to win this one too.

Chip worked himself out of the hole, and the score remained 3-3 until the top of the eighth when Soapy misjudged one of Chip's breaking pitches. The ball struck him on the thumb. Soapy dropped his catcher's glove and grabbed his right hand.

Chip called time and hurried to home plate, where he was joined by Rockwell, Pop Brown, and Doc Jones.

Soapy's thumb had already started to swell; it hung loose and helpless. Soapy wasn't crying wolf this time. He was really hurt. Chip and the rest of the Big Reds stood helplessly by and heard Doc Jones say regretfully, "It's broken, Rock!"

Carl Carey came trotting in from right field to catch, and Chip went back to the mound with a sad heart. The injury to Soapy hurt. And it had a bad effect on every

STRIKE THREE!

player on the team too. Edgemont took advantage of the situation to load the bases again. Chip got out of that trouble by a force play at the plate and a scintillating double play by Speed and Cody. In the last of the ninth, Ted Williams banged out a double that scored Morris, and the game was over. Final score: Valley Falls 4, Edgemont 3.

At Steeltown, the Iron Men defeated Weston easily, and now everything depended upon Saturday's game. Steeltown and Valley Falls were still tied for the section championship, each with eight victories and two defeats.

There wasn't much fun around the Sugar Bowl that night or in the next two days. Soapy kept his chin up and tried to laugh off his injury, but deep inside he was sick and hurt.

Chip's happiness got a jolt too. Petey Jackson told him that Buck Adams and Peck Weaver were betting anyone in town that Steeltown would win the game on Saturday.

Chip's mind was in turmoil. The old doubts about Carl Carey returned, although Carl gave no indication he was doing anything other than playing to win. He worked hard in practice and was enthusiastic and friendly with Chip.

Rockwell and his two assistants also were greatly worried because of the loss of Soapy. Now everything depended upon an inexperienced catcher and one over-worked pitcher. Rockwell had hoped Lefty Peters would be ready for these end-of-the-season games, but Doc Jones dashed those hopes.

The Valley Falls fans weren't alarmed. They were counting on Chip Hilton. And that was welcome music to the ears of Buck Adams and Peck Weaver.

INTEGRITY ON THE HILL

On Friday, at the pottery, in the stores, and on the streets, the chief topic of conversation was the upcoming game. In every home that night, the subject was baseball. The Carey house was small and perched high on the South Side Hill. It was home, the center of everything in the world, to the close-knit family. Mrs. Carey, Ken, Carl, and the twelve-year-old twins, Kate and Luke, sat on the porch that evening and talked about the game and Carl's role in the big event.

Ken gradually withdrew from the conversation and, as the evening shadows slowly gathered, watched his mother's happy face with a sick heart. Ken was the head of this family; he had assumed that responsibility years ago, sacrificing his own ambitions by quitting school to go to work. His earnings at the pottery took care of the family's expenses, and now his greatest desire was to put the twins and Carl through school.

Later, he and Carl walked up the broad wooden steps that led to the Hill. Two streets above, they paused on one of the landings and turned to look across the river to the West Side where the lights flickered on one by one.

Carl and Ken had always been close. Now Carl sensed that something was troubling his brother. "What's wrong, Ken?" he asked.

Ken didn't reply, and after a short silence Carl spoke again. "You're not in with Peck's crowd, are you, Ken?" he asked anxiously.

"No, I'm not doing any betting, Carl, but—"

"Are they mad 'cause you stuck up for Chip, for Hilton?"

"No, Carl, it's—it's something else."

"I'm glad it's not Hilton, Ken. He's OK. He has to work and everything, and he's proud as can be, but he's a regular guy. We were all wrong about him, Ken. Nick was, too, but he's too stubborn to admit it. If it isn't Chip, what is it, Ken?"

"Nothing. Skip it!"

"But I don't want to skip it, Ken. It's about time I began helping out at home and helping you too. I'm not going to see you pushed around by *anyone!*"

As the two brothers stood there leaning against the guard rail of the steps, each was busy with his own personal problem. Carl had idolized his brother for years. He loved Ken for the sacrifices he had made and was making to keep the family going.

Ken had a much greater problem. One that meant much to the Carey family in a lot of ways. He had to make a decision tonight, a big decision. Either way, it might mean the loss of his job and, with that loss, much unhappiness to the entire family. Buck Adams and Peck Weaver's demands were unbearable. They were trying to force Carl to betray all the ideals sports stood for and all the integrity that was the pride of the Hill crowd.

Suddenly, Ken was sick of everything about his association with Buck Adams and Peck Weaver. He sighed deeply but thankfully. He had made up his mind. He might lose the respect of everyone on the Hill because of a cowardly incident years ago, but he didn't intend to betray his brother or mess up Carl's chance to escape the limitations of life on the Hill.

Ken placed his arm roughly around Carl's shoulder.

"I guess you think I'm crazy, Carl. And maybe I am. But I want Valley Falls to win that game tomorrow more than I've ever wanted anything in my life! And that covers a lot of ground. Give 'em all you've got tomorrow, Carl. Work with that Hilton kid as you never worked with anyone in your life! You've got to win that game for *me!*"

INTEGRITY ON THE HILL

Main Street in Valley Falls did more business on Saturday than all the rest of the week combined. But not this Saturday. Nearly everyone in Valley Falls was jammed in the grandstand or the bleachers at Ohlsen Field. This was the ball game of the year, and the fans meant to see it!

They saw a game all right. It was a pitcher's battle from the time the umpire roared, "Play ball!" until the last inning. Chip and Charles Minor, Steeltown's pitching star, had each pitched perfect ball for seven innings. Each had given up two hits. And now, in the bottom of the seventh, with the score 1-1, two down, and Chris Badger perched on second base, Carl Carey was up.

The noise was terrific. All the Valley Falls fans were on their feet yelling for Carl Carey. Carl's face was drawn and pale, but his eyes were steady. This was his chance! His chance to win for Ken!

Minor was clever. He kept the ball low and outside. But Carl had a keen eye and watched the pitches for the full count. Chip was on deck, anxious to get up there, anxious to win his own game. But he never got the chance. Carey met the fat, three-two pitch on the nose, and the ball sailed over second base.

Soapy was coaching at third base, and with the hit he ran toward home waving his bandaged thumb like a windmill. You could even hear Soapy above the din of the delirious crowd, yelling, "Come on, Chris! Slide! Slide! Slide!"

Badger rounded third and tore for home and the championship of Section Two. Chip sent a swift glance at the ball, which was flying in on a perfect line. Then he dropped his bat and palmed his hands toward the ground. This was going to be close.

"Slide, Chris, slide!" he yelled.

STRIKE THREE!

Badger came in charging, oblivious to everything except the Steeltown catcher and the plate. The ball came in on a long, low bounce straight into the catcher's waiting glove. A split second later, two hundred pounds and eighteen years of tough Hill training crashed head-first into the Iron Men's receiver.

The Steeltown catcher was knocked ten feet behind the plate, and the ball flew out of his glove and up in the air as Badger slid flat on his stomach across the plate.

Chip's anxious eyes saw the umpire poised in a squat with his arms wide to his sides and with the palms of his hands flat to the ground. Badger was in, and the Big Reds were in!

CHAPTER 22

Sink or Swim

THE SUGAR BOWL did record business that night, and Petey Jackson was kept busy until nine o'clock. As soon as the rush slackened, Petey asked Chip to take his place behind the counter for a few minutes and dashed back to the storeroom for his windbreaker.

"What's the big rush? Where you going?" Chip asked.

"Got business. Big business!" Petey whispered in Chip's ear. "I gotta go down and collect! Old Leroy missed the boat again!"

In a few minutes Petey was back.

"There's a lot of trouble brewing down at Sorelli's. Buck Adams and Peck Weaver are angry at Ken Carey about something. Everyone's talkin' about the big argument they had—"

Everybody was talking about Valley Falls and the state championship too. That night, Soapy waited around to help Chip and Petey close up. The sweeping and dusting were finished quickly, and Petey hurried off for his usual game of pool. A little later, Chip and Soapy started home together. Just as they passed the main entrance of the Academy, the side door of Sorelli's crashed open and three men hurtled into the alley. Their angry voices carried all the way across the street.

"That's Weaver and Adams," Chip whispered.

"Yeah, and they're yelling at Ken Carey. Look at that!"

The loud talk broke off suddenly, and Adams and Weaver both closed in on Carey. Ken didn't have a chance. He was trying to defend himself, but Adams and Weaver hammered blow after blow upon him. He was pinned helplessly against the Academy wall while a crowd of onlookers stood in stunned silence watching the unequal contest.

Chip couldn't stand it. "Come on, Soapy," he said angrily. "I can't watch that!"

Soapy grabbed Chip's arm with his good hand. "No, Chip! Stay out of it."

But Chip jerked himself free and dashed across the street. Soapy followed, tightening his belt and moaning, "Oh, my poor thumb! Here we go! My poor thumb!"

Chip smashed through the crowd of bewildered onlookers and hit Peck Weaver with a shoulder block that knocked the surprised man to his knees. Soapy went even further. He tackled Buck Adams viciously around the knees and simply held on. Adams couldn't do a thing and couldn't get out of Soapy's grip although he kicked and twisted with all his strength.

It was different with Weaver and Chip. They went to it. Peck scrambled to his feet and rushed Chip.

"So it's you again," he gritted. "Well, this time—"

But that was as far as Weaver got. This time Chip didn't wait. He met Peck's rush with a right that packed in every ounce of his weight and power.

SINK OR SWIM

Chip's fist fully contacted Weaver's jaw and turned the bulky roughneck around. Peck staggered headfirst against the side of the building, and before he could turn, Chip seized the opportunity to clamp his long arms around the bully's body. Then he forced Weaver up against the side of the Academy and held him there.

While Chip and Weaver were battling, Ken Carey had time to recover. He started tugging at Soapy, trying to pull him off Adams. Ken wanted to fight it out with Buck himself, but Soapy wasn't letting go. He had Adams harnessed and meant to keep him that way. Then Petey Jackson got into the fracas, tugging at Chip and Weaver. The rest of the crowd, which had done nothing up to this point, came to its senses and pulled the men and boys apart and broke up the fight.

"We'll see *you* later, Carey," Weaver snarled, rubbing his swollen jaw.

"Yeah," Adams added, "we have unfinished business with *you!*"

But Ken Carey didn't hear. Chip, Soapy, and Petey had pulled him away, and they were walking as one up the street.

"Come to my house," Chip urged. "You can clean up and rest."

Mrs. Hilton's usually calm face showed surprise and concern when Chip, Soapy, and Petey entered with Ken Carey. Ken's face was bruised and cut in several places, and his clothes were dirty and torn.

"What happened to—" she began, but a glance at Chip's grim face stopped her questions and she went into action. "Take him out in the kitchen, Chip," she said. "I'll get something to clean up those cuts."

Mrs. Hilton went to get the first aid kit, and Chip asked Ken if he thought he'd have trouble going home.

STRIKE THREE!

"I'll have trouble, all right," Ken said wearily. "I'll have trouble tonight and a lot of nights!"

"We'll go home with you," Soapy declared. "We'll take you home. I'm going to call Biggie and Abe!"

"No, I don't think that would be wise," Ken said slowly. "I believe I can make it all right by myself."

After Mary Hilton treated Ken's cuts, Soapy plundered the refrigerator and brought in a tray filled with snacks into the family room. Any excuse to eat! Mrs. Hilton had Chip explain what had happened. Moments later, the telephone rang. An anxious Carl Carey was on the other end.

"Is Ken there, Chip?"

"Sure, Carl. He's right here."

Ken Carey's jaw tightened, and he breathed deeply as he took the receiver. "Hi ya, Carl. . . . Sure, sure I'm all right. . . . Yes, but I'm all right. It's not necessary. . . . OK, I'll wait!"

Carey hung up the phone and turned to Chip. "Carl's coming over, Chip. Do you mind, Mrs. Hilton?"

"Of course not!"

Minutes later, Carl Carey came running up the front steps. Chip met him at the front door.

"Where's Ken? How is he? I've come to take him home!"

"We'll go with you," Chip said in a low voice. "Just in case you meet Adams and Weaver."

"We won't meet them," Carl said with a knowing wink. "That's all set!" He jerked his head toward the kitchen. "Mind if I talk to Ken privately a minute?"

As the two brothers went into the kitchen, Chip rejoined his mom, Soapy, and Petey. A few minutes later, Carl called Chip.

"Chip, Ken wants to talk to you."

Sitting at the kitchen table, Chip listened with amazement as Ken Carey related the plot that Buck

SINK OR SWIM

Adams and Peck Weaver had cooked up to win money on the Valley Falls High School baseball games. They had purposely worked on Carl and Nick all through the early practices and during the season, developing an animosity for Chip Hilton. Ken had been drawn into the scheme a little at a time without realizing how far the two crooks had planned to go. But when they demanded that Ken force Carl and Nick to throw the games and make Valley Falls lose, he had rebelled. That was wrong. Adams had suggested that Ken get Carl to make bad throws to the bases or let a pitched ball get away from him at strategic times against Steeltown.

Chip turned toward Carl.

"Carl never knew anything about it, Chip!" Ken exclaimed. "Neither did Nick! Peck and Buck used what they called psychology to create a grudge between you guys. I guess I might as well tell you the whole story while I'm at it. You ought to know why I got myself into such a mess and into such bad company.

"I never liked Buck Adams and Peck Weaver, but there was a reason for our apparent friendship. A long time ago, when I was a kid, I used to go over back of the Hill with a boy named Leroy White and play in the creek. One day, we decided the creek was small stuff and we went to the river. There was a big group there, playing around the rocks and the broken-down engines on the old railroad spur, and we joined them. They drifted off, and only Leroy and me were left.

"Neither of us could swim but Leroy could dive, and his favorite thing was to jump from one rock to another. We were standing on the edge of the water, and suddenly Leroy took a run and dove headfirst toward one of the rocks. But he must have got a cramp or hit bottom because he yelled for help. I couldn't swim a stroke so I did the only thing I knew to do. I ran for help, hollering at the top of my voice. Buck Adams and Peck Weaver heard me and came running and pulled Leroy out of the water.

"Buck and Peck were older than Leroy and me and were good swimmers. They made fun of me that day and called me a coward. A short time after that, Leroy moved away, but Buck and Peck never forgot."

Ken paused a moment and then continued reflectively: "The South Side is no place for a coward. The guys are tough over there, and they don't go for cowards.

"Weaver and Adams have held that near-drowning incident over my head for years. Naturally—foolishly, too, I suppose—I didn't want anyone to know about it. Those two have used it as a club to get me to do things— nothing bad or wrong—but little things that helped them further their own ends. The only thing I'm afraid of now is that I'll lose my job. Buck Adams's father is my boss at the pottery."

"You won't lose your job," Carl said quietly. "We've got a little surprise waiting for those two guys. Come on! We've got to go!"

"What's going on?" Ken asked suspiciously.

"Nothing," Carl said grimly, "nothing except Nick, Chris, and Cody and about fifty other guys are waiting over by the bridge for Buck and Peck to bother us! Then those two are gonna get a real Hill surprise!"

"How did they find out about it so quickly?" Chip asked.

Carl smiled, but it wasn't a humorous expression. His eyes were too hard, his jaw too square. "I told Ken about that out in the kitchen. You see, Buck and Peck stopped me tonight on the bridge right after the fight and told me about Ken and Leroy White. They said Ken was a coward and was their partner in the whole deal and he had double-crossed them. But I knew better!

"You see, Chip, Ken told me last night to try my hardest to win this game, and by the way he said it, I knew something was wrong.

"Well, anyway, when they stopped me on the bridge and told me all that nonsense, I decided to tell Nick, Chris, and Cody about it. And I did! Then the first thing I knew, some of Ken's pals from the pottery heard about the fight and they got mad, and now they're all waiting over there in the alley behind Carroll's store."

Ken Carey shook his head. "This gang stuff is not for us or our family. I don't like that, Carl. I'd rather take care of my own problems."

Carl placed a hand on his brother's shoulder. "You're right about the gang stuff. But your problems are my problems, too, Ken. That's what little brothers are for. From now on, we'll sink or swim together!"

CHAPTER 23

University, Here We Come!

THOSE FIVE days after the Steeltown game seemed like five months to Chip. But noon of that hot Thursday, June 23, finally arrived. It seemed that half the town turned out for the Big Reds send-off.

Final exams had finished only that morning, but the entire student body was gathered on the gym steps and on the lawn and in the street around the bus. The Big Reds band was there, sounding exuberant but looking wilted in its uniforms. Principal Zimmerman made a short speech. When he finished, the perspiring band formed in the street, and with the bus following in low gear, everyone joined in a parade down Main Street. University, here they come!

Chip Hilton sat with Carl Carey. The catcher told his blond seatmate about what had happened after he and Ken had left Chip's house a few days before.

"Then there wasn't any trouble?"

"I'll say there wasn't," replied Carl. "Adams and Weaver showed the white flag the minute they saw us. Lucky for them they did too! I had to hand it to Ken. He sure told 'em off! Chief Cummings turned up about then and ordered Buck and Peck to stay off the Hill—for keeps!"

Chip nodded. "Carl, I'm glad it all turned out all right."

"Chip," said Carey, as the bus moved through the cheering crowds along the street, "the coach looks worried!"

"Coaches always look worried, Carl. He's worried that we'll win tomorrow's game and that we'll run out of pitchers. He won't let me go twice in two days."

"What do you think you have, an invincible arm?" said Carey with a laugh and a good-natured shove.

University was packed. It seemed to Chip that every coach and every baseball fan in the state was there, standing on corners and in little groups around town talking about the upcoming games. Rockwell had arranged for the Valley Falls group to stay at the same hotel that had housed the Big Reds when they had won the basketball title, and they were all assigned rooms on the tenth floor.

Chip, Paddy, Speed, and Biggie drew a two-room suite, and Soapy and Carl were right across the hall. Paddy threw his glove, bat, and bag on one of the twin beds and headed for the window. He had never been so high up in the air in his life. The little bat boy was thrilled. It was his first trip away from home.

Chip unpacked and then looked at Paddy leaning out the window. Paddy was unusually quiet. Chip watched him intently. He wasn't sure that he saw what he suspected.

"Hey," he called. "You squirting people out that window? Down on the street?"

STRIKE THREE!

Paddy's head shot around, and he shook it vigorously. "Uh-uh. Not me. Not missin' by much though," he giggled, hiding the yellow squirt gun behind his tiny back.

"Well, you cut it out. They'll throw us out of this hotel and out of the series too! Do you want to stay with Soapy?"

Paddy reluctantly canceled further water practice. "No way! When do we eat?" he asked.

"Not until seven o'clock."

"Well, then, let's practice." Paddy grabbed his glove and ball from the bed.

"Can't. We've got a skull practice in half an hour."

Paddy regarded Chip doubtfully. "Skull practice? Who you kiddin'? I think you're teasing me."

Paddy was still doubtful when the squad assembled a little later in the banquet hall. But Rockwell ended all his doubts.

"We meet Rutledge tomorrow afternoon at three o'clock. It's a good draw. Edgemont meets Coreyville in the top half of the draw at eleven o'clock. We'll go to that game together in the bus and leave early for a light lunch at 12:15. Dinner tonight, seven o'clock. After that, you're free until 10:30. Be in your room at 10:30 and lights out at eleven. Paddy, you're with the coaches until lights out.

"By the way, Chet has movie tickets for everyone. Have a good time!"

Chip didn't go to the movie. After a short walk, he bought a paper and went up to his room. As he unlocked his door, he was surprised to see Carl Carey's door open across the hall.

"Didn't you go to the show?" Chip asked.

Carl shook his head. "No, Chip. I didn't feel like it. Mind if I come in? That is, if you're not busy. . . ."

"I'm sure not busy. Except for thinking about the game tomorrow."

Carl nodded. "Me too! I'm scared stiff, Chip. I've been dreamin' and hopin' for this, and here I am worried sick the night before the game. Suppose I don't hold up?"

"You'll hold up all right!" Chip said confidently. "Everybody's a little nervous the night before a big game like this! My stomach's full of butterflies!"

Carl nodded his head doubtfully and then gazed out the window reflectively. After a short silence, he cleared his throat. "Chip," he said hesitantly, "I've been wondering what the Rock's gonna do for pitching if we win tomorrow. Cody said he heard Rock tell Stewart he was gonna pitch Williams if we won the Rutledge game."

"I've been wondering about it, too, Carl. I'd like to pitch both games, but I don't think Coach will let me do it. I sure wish Lefty was here. But Doc Jones said Lefty couldn't do anything this summer. If only Nick—"

"That's just what I was thinking, Chip. Ya think Rock'd give Nick another chance?"

Before Chip could reply, Carl continued quickly, "Nick's a good guy, Chip. He just got in wrong because of Adams and Weaver." Carl's face clouded, and his voice was bitter as he added, "Those two guys really took advantage of us and—"

"I know, Carl," Chip said understandingly. "Skip it."

There was a long silence in the room. Each boy was busy with his own thoughts. Chip was thinking about Trullo—that first day when Nick had tried to bean him, the crossed signs, the angry pitch in the Southern game that sent a player to the hospital, bad throws with men on base to make Chip look bad, sarcastic digs about "coach's pet" and "snitcher," the reception on the Hill . . . .

Chip's jaw was set hard when he broke the silence. "You think Nick's in shape, Carl?"

STRIKE THREE!

"Sure, Chip!" Carl said eagerly. "I know Nick's in shape! He's been pitching almost every evening on the Hill."

Chip picked up the paper and studied the pairing of the teams.

FRIDAY

| 11:00 A.M. | Edgemont vs. Coreyville |
| 3:00 P.M. | Rutledge vs. Valley Falls |

SATURDAY

| 11:00 A.M. | Third place game |
| 3:00 P.M. | Championship game |

He figured the Rock would start him against Rutledge. The Ruts had a record of 16 and 1. Valley Falls had already beaten Edgemont 4-3, and even though the Big Reds had lost to Coreyville 19-8, that game had been Soapy's first experience as a pitcher. It stood to reason the coach would start Chip tomorrow. Besides, there wouldn't be a championship game for the Big Reds if they didn't beat Rutledge, and Valley Falls wasn't exactly loaded with pitchers.

"I'll do it!" Chip said, half to himself and half to Carey. "I've got to do it!"

There wasn't much sleep for Chip that night. Try as hard as he could, sleep wouldn't come. He was groggy the next morning and felt lifeless while watching Coreyville take the lead against Edgemont. Right after the team lunch, the Big Reds got the final score: Coreyville 6, Edgemont 2. At least they knew who one of the finalists was going to be.

CHAPTER 24

Another and Another and Another

SOAPY SMITH dramatically waved his broken thumb in a circle. "We'll be running things up here in a couple of years," he boasted. He looked around the room, trying to get an assistant for his act. But there was no response. The happy comedian was the only person in the room who wasn't pale and tense. The Big Reds were pulling on their uniforms, tying up their cleats, and nervously adjusting their caps in dead silence. The small group of athletes barely filled one corner of the big locker room in the depths of University Field House.

Chip thought about Soapy's words. Yes, he realized, some of the guys would be up here in a year or two. He would be, too, if he got some sort of scholarship or was able to save more money.

"All right, pay attention!"

Rockwell, standing in the center of the locker room, was wearing his snug baseball suit. The broken bill of his old baseball cap was pulled far down over his right eye. Chet Stewart and Bill Thomas, dressed in Valley Falls uniforms, stood behind the veteran coach.

"We're off to a good start. We won the toss, and so we'll get last hits at bat. Here's the batting order: Collins, Morris, Williams, Cohen, Schwartz, Badger, Rodriguez, Carey, and Hilton. Now, hustle out on the field and get a good warm-up. This is it!"

The grandstand and the bleachers were jammed when the players reached the diamond. Between warm-up pitches to Carey, Chip let his gaze wander around the field. Over by the Valley Falls dugout, he saw a familiar figure. It was Del Bennett! He caught Chip's eye and walked out to the practice rubber.

"Hello, Hilton. I see you got your wish! Been following you in the papers. Nice work."

A few minutes later, Chip was standing in front of the dugout and heard the umpire announcing:

"Ladies and Gentlemen, the batteries for today's game, for Rutledge: Cowles and Newcombe. For Valley Falls: Hilton and Carey. P-L-A-Y B-A-L-L!"

Chip kicked the dust in front of the rubber a couple of times and then blazed his warm-up pitches down the alley. His tired feeling was gone. Del Bennett's words had energized him! But talk wouldn't help him now. He concentrated on Carl's target. Now it was up to him!

The first Rut was the skinny little second baseman. He crowded the plate with his needlelike elbows, and Chip didn't have the heart to move him back with a close one. Before he knew it, the batter had worked him for a base on balls. Chip could have kicked himself for walking the first batter to face him.

Before he could regain his poise and get his thoughts off the bad start, Rutledge had sacrificed its leadoff man down to second, and the power hitters were up. Then Chip began to bear down. He wasn't going to get behind one of those strong hitters! They spelled trouble. All teams concentrate their good hitters in the third, fourth, and fifth spots.

Chip got the edge on the next hitter with two straight called strikes, then a foul, a ball, another foul, a ball, and then he blazed his fastball right across the inside corner for the third strike. Chip figured the next batter, the cleanup hitter, would take one. Right then, one of the things Coach Bennett had told him about trying to outguess a hitter came true. The Rutledge power hitter met the pitch right on the nose and drove a line shot between Schwartz and Rodriguez. It was a triple, and Rutledge was out in front with a run. Chip stopped guessing!

There was no more scoring for seven innings. Cowles, a stocky two-hundred-pounder, was blazing a hopping fastball right past the Big Reds. Every inning, Paddy, Soapy, Pop, Chet, and Bill Thomas said, "This is the big inning," but it wasn't. Chip looked as bad as the rest of Valley Falls at the plate. Cowles's right-hand fastballs were what Chip liked, but he never made solid contact.

Badger outlasted Cowles in the bottom of the seventh and walked on the sixth pitch. Rockwell was worried now. This game was nearly over. He had to try for the tying run. Mike Rodriguez put down a perfect bunt along the third-base line, and although the throw to first got him by a step, his sacrifice advanced Chris to second. The Big Reds dugout was praying for a hit when Carey came to bat.

Carl slashed into the first pitch and drove it down the third-base line. Badger moved with the hit but pulled up quickly when the third baseman made a marvelous one-hand stop. Chris barely beat the throw back to second. But he and Carl were both safe, and Chip was up with a chance to win his own game.

Chip dropped the extra bats he had been swinging and walked around to the first-base side of the batter's box. Then before stepping up to the plate, he cast a quick look down at Speed in the third-base coaching box. But there was no sign, and Chip realized he was being given the green light. He was on his own.

Cowles pitched carefully to Chip but got behind, three and one. The next pitch was in there, all right, and Chip took a full cut. He got a piece of it but was too far under, and the ball went spinning high into the air. His heart sank when he heard the umpire call, "Infield fly!"

Chip ran it out although he knew it was no use. He was automatically out whether the ball was caught or not. The shortstop made the catch, and Chip walked slowly back to the dugout, mentally scolding himself every step of the way. He had put too much into that swing, had tried to kill the ball. All he had to do was make contact with the ball. A missed opportunity. What a chump!

Now it was two down, men on first and second, and Cody Collins at bat. Everyone in the Valley Falls dugout was pleading for the stocky second baseman to "bring 'em in" and yelling for Chris and Carl to "run on anything!"

Cody didn't bring them both in but did get hold of one of Cowles's darting curves. It was a Texas leaguer, right over the shortstop's head, and Chris Badger, on his way with the crack of the bat, tore around third and headed for home. Red Schwartz had replaced Morris in the third-base coaching box and waved Chris toward home. The Rutledge left fielder gunned the ball home, but Chris beat the throw and slid across the plate with the tying tally. Then Morris went down swinging for the third out. But the Big Reds were happy as they scampered out on the field.

ANOTHER AND ANOTHER AND ANOTHER

And so the game went, inning after inning, a pitchers' duel, with the 1-1 on the scoreboard followed by a row of goose eggs until the bottom of the fourteenth.

Morris led off and tried to work Cowles for a walk. But Cowles was too smart to get behind and struck Speed out. Williams hadn't hit the ball all day, but he doubled on the first pitch, and Biggie Cohen was up with a chance to empty the stands. Soapy and Paddy were praying for Biggie to "clear the pond," and it seemed that the crowd was in the same mood. For a minute, it even looked as if Biggie was going to do it. He was batting left-handed and pulled Cowles's third pitch high in the air toward the right-field fence. Ted Williams, on second, watched the ball for an instant and then started for third. But Cody Collins, in the third-base coaching box, waved him back. The Rutledge right fielder, camped just short of the fence, hauled in Biggie's long out. Ted had tagged up by this time and hurried toward third on the catch. He beat the throw easily. So with two down and the score still tied, Schwartz was up.

Little Paddy took the extra bat out of Schwartz's hands and then hooked a left fist into Red's stomach. "Come on," he whined. "I'm tired! I wanna go home! I'm hungry!"

Red sent them all home! He met Cowles's second pitch with a slashing single over second base that sent Ted Williams sprinting home with the winning run.

The Big Reds celebrated at dinner that night. But in the team meeting at 7:30, Rockwell advised his athletes that they hadn't come to University to celebrate anything but the championship. That quieted them down.

A little later, Chet Stewart looked down in amazement at the handful of movie tickets he held. Not a single player had asked for a ticket. If he had checked Chip's room, he would have understood why. Every member of the squad was there. The chief topic was, of course, tomorrow's game and the question of who would be the starting pitcher.

Chip was deep in thought. He had heard the phone ring several times but had paid no attention when Soapy answered. This time, however, when the phone rang and Soapy answered, he was puzzled. Soapy listened a second, said, "It sure is," and then hung up.

"What's that all about?" Chip asked.

Soapy laughed. "Someone's trying to play a joke on me for once, I guess. They keep saying, 'Long-distance from Valley Falls!' So, I agree with them. *It is* a long distance from Valley Falls! Some wise guy, huh?"

That did it. Rockwell's sobering influence vanished like one of Petey Jackson's ice-cream sundaes. The players piled all over Soapy, and the next two hours were spent in the usual bantering, needling, and joking. During the good-natured clowning and fooling around, which included flying pillows and Paddy's squirt gun, Chip was busy with his thoughts and plans. At ten o'clock, the roughhousing broke up, and only Speed, Biggie, Ted, and Paddy were left with Chip. Chip closed the door and faced the group.

"Look, guys," he began, "I've been thinking about tomorrow's game. I know the Rock isn't going to let me pitch, and since none of you want to, I was thinking the best solution might be to go to the coach and try to get him to give Nick Trullo another chance."

Chip paused and looked intently at his friends' faces. No one said a word. Biggie found something wrong with his shoestring. Speed suddenly became interested in seeing that Paddy brushed his teeth a second time before going to bed, and Ted Williams picked up a newspaper.

"Well," Chip demanded, "what's so terrible about that?"

Still, there was only silence. Chip pulled the paper out of Ted's hands and directed his remarks straight to the quiet senior. "You're the captain of this team, Ted. It's your responsibility! Seems to me I remember you going to the Rock about Nick crossing up the signs. I don't see why you can't or won't go to him now, when there's a state championship at stake!"

Ted looked at Chip with kind, patient eyes but shook his head. "Not me, Chip. I don't want to win a state championship that badly. Nick ran out on us. Well, in my mind, that ends the matter!"

"Yeah," Speed added, as he paused in the door leading to the adjoining bedroom. "We've come this far without Trullo, and we can go on without him!"

"Those are my sentiments," Biggie said quietly. "Guess I'll call it a night. 'Night, everybody." He followed Speed into their room and softly closed the door.

Ted got slowly to his feet and placed a hand on Chip's shoulder. "I'm sorry, Chip," he said. "I just can't see it! I wish I could—for your sake. See ya later."

Paddy came out of the bathroom in a pair of Petey's striped pajamas. Speed had turned them up to the little fellow's knees, and the sleeves were rolled up under his skinny arms so he looked as if he were wearing a pair of shoulder pads.

"Come on, Chip," he said. "You'll have to pitch tomorrow. You know what the coach said. Lights out!"

Chip snapped off the lights and began to undress. But he paused after he had removed one shoe and sat motionless. Then he put the shoe on again and tiptoed softly out of the room.

Down at the end of the hall in Room 1033, Rockwell, Stewart, Pop, and Bill Thomas were holding a last-minute strategy meeting. When Chip knocked on the door and heard Rockwell's call to enter, he paused with surprise. "I'm sorry, Coach," he said. "I thought you were alone."

"That's all right, Chip. Come in."

"But I . . . I . . ."

Stewart got to his feet. "Well, good night, Coach. We'd better go to bed. Come on, Bill, Pop."

Chip sat down on a chair and faced a waiting Rockwell.

"What's on your mind, Chip?"

"Coach, I was thinking about tomorrow's game and wondering if . . . wondering who was going to pitch—"

Chip looked at Rockwell questioningly and then continued hopefully, "I was hoping you would let me try it."

"No, Chip, I'd never let a pitcher start two days in a row. You ought to know that. I might use him for an inning or so the second day, but I'd never let him pitch two full games in two days. I don't want to win that badly!"

"But it's for the championship, Coach. And my arm feels great!"

"The answer is no, Chip. We'll use Williams or Schwartz and hope for the best. Neither one has much on the ball, but we'll try to get some runs for them. I expect to use you in the outfield though, if that'll make you feel any better."

Chip sighed resignedly and then got to the real purpose of his visit. He spoke rapidly and to the point. He told Rockwell all about Adams and Weaver and Ken Carey, and about Buck and Peck using mind games and scheming to instigate hate between Nick, Carl, and himself. Then he told Rockwell about the final showdown and what had happened to Adams and Weaver after the fight.

"Nick wasn't to blame, Coach. You know how it is over on the South Side. Every guy over there has to stand up for his rights and fight his own battles. Nick just got a bad break. He wasn't any different from Carl. He thought it was smart to act tough and to hate fellows like me who live on the West Side. You just have to give him another chance, Coach. Just have to! He deserves it! It means the championship!"

Rockwell said nothing until Chip finished. Then the hard lines around his mouth and eyes relaxed, and he leaned forward and spoke softly to the anxious boy.

"Chip, I appreciate your interest in the team and your desire to do anything and everything you can to see Valley Falls win the honors and the championship tomorrow. But every once in a while a coach has to make decisions that can't be influenced by championships and honors. Nick Trullo had every chance to show some semblance of manhood and an understanding of fair play. But at no time did he make the slightest effort to sacrifice his own feelings for the team. In fact, practically everything he did hurt the team.

"Why, Chip, I couldn't give somebody like that another chance. He's not entitled to it.

"Nick Trullo never showed any regret whatever for his actions. Never made a single move to show he realized his mistakes. You surely don't expect me to ask him to come back to the team just because we need a pitcher and there's a championship at stake. I thought you knew me better than that!"

"I know how you feel, Coach, but Nick does realize his mistake. I know he does! He probably feels the same way you do—feels he can't come to you now that the team is doing so well without him. I know Nick pretty well, even though we don't get along. I know he's all right!"

Rockwell knew boys. He knew this one about as well as he had ever known any. And he liked this one about as much as he had ever liked any. He wanted to soften his refusal as much as possible. Then he had an idea.

"But Trullo hasn't been pitching, Chipper. He wouldn't be any use to us if he's not in shape. And it wouldn't be fair to him to put him in a situation like that unprepared."

"But he is in shape, Coach. Carl says Nick has been playing almost every night up on the Hill. I know he's in shape, Coach."

A grim little smile played about the corners of Rockwell's mouth. He wasn't getting very far in this debate. The kid had all the answers.

"Well, Chip," he said, "you go to bed and let me think it over. Perhaps by morning I'll feel differently. You've done all you can. Now get some rest."

But Rockwell couldn't sleep. He called Chet Stewart, and the two coaches went for a long walk. Rockwell told Stewart the story.

"Why, Rock," Stewart said, "always and always I've heard you say a kid was entitled to another chance. You aren't going back on that, are you? After all these years?"

"But, Chet, I don't think this one is a good kid. I gave him every opportunity—"

"But, Rock, another chance means another chance and another and another, doesn't it? Trullo is a hard-boiled kid on the surface. But how do we know what kind of person he is deep down under that South Side shell? I say, call him tonight! Besides, when have *you* ever given up on a kid?"

Long after Stewart had gone to bed, Rockwell debated the problem. And when he finally closed his eyes with a deep sigh of fatigue, he had reached a decision.

CHAPTER 25

The Prodigal Pitcher

COACH ROCKWELL wasn't the only person to have a restless night. Chip barely slept. And to make it worse, Paddy was up at the crack of dawn, leaning out the window and whistling at people on the sidewalk. At eight o'clock the phone rang. It was Rockwell.

"Do you think your mother could get in touch with Nick Trullo, Chip?"

Chip's hopes leaped. "Sure, Coach. She'll get him. I'll call her at her office."

"How will Trullo get here?"

"Why, why, Mr. Schroeder will drive him over, Coach. I'll have Mom call him too."

A few minutes later, Mary Hilton was trying to understand just what Chip needed—Nick Trullo had to be found and had to be driven to University. It meant the *championship,* and it was all up to her!

STRIKE THREE!

Mary Hilton had her hands full. Nick Trullo's family had no phone. She didn't even know where the Trullos lived! But she figured Doc Jones would know. After all, he knew everyone and where everyone in Valley Falls lived. Doc agreed with Mary Hilton. This was a serious matter, an emergency, and John Schroeder should be called to help in the effort.

Fifteen minutes later, Schroeder was holding on to the car dash with one hand and the door handle with the other as Doc Jones hit every bump across the bridge and straight up the Hill to the last street near the crest. Jones knew these families better than anyone else, and he was about the only West-Sider the Hill people completely trusted. They were entirely unselfish in their praise and regard for the good doctor. Doc had never turned down a sick call from the South Side, and he never sent a bill to anyone who couldn't pay.

Mamma Trullo was overjoyed to see Doc Jones. Nick? Oh, that Nick! No, she didn't know where they could find her grandson. But he'd be home at noon; he never missed a meal!

With resigned sighs, the guardians of Valley Falls's championship hopes sat down and waited for Nick. Just as the Valley Falls Pottery siren announced noon, Nick Trullo and Ken Carey were on the porch. Doc Jones opened the door and blurted, "Nick, Coach Rockwell sent word for you to hurry up to University! He wants you to pitch the championship game this afternoon! Come with us, and we'll get you something to eat on the way!"

Jones grabbed the surprised teenager by the arm, but Trullo shook his head and pulled away. "That's real funny, Doc. Rockwell wouldn't send for me. Besides, what's the matter with Hilton? He's doin' all right!"

THE PRODIGAL PITCHER

And Nick stuck to it. Nothing Jones or Schroeder could say or do would change his mind. Ken had been watching and listening intently. Now he interrupted. "Let me talk to Nick," he said.

He pulled a protesting Nick aside. "Look, Nick," Ken began, "you've got to go! This is your chance. You and I know better than anyone else, I guess, that we've been wrong about this baseball deal. And, besides, Carl's in on this too. And if the Rock is sending for you . . . well, it seems to me you ought to be man enough to go!"

Nick was wavering, and Ken followed the advantage. "Look, Nick, the whole South Side is hoping Valley Falls will win this game. Think what it would mean if you and Carl could team up and do it. C'mon, let's go!"

Ken didn't use any further arguments. He simply grabbed Nick by the arm and shoved him around the car and into the seat. They were on their way!

Doc skillfully maneuvered the car down the winding, narrow streets off the Hill, going as fast as he could. But his thoughts were racing miles faster than his old car's limit. He turned to John Schroeder.

"We'll never make it in this thing, John," he said. "It's 12:10, and University's about three hours away. Can't be done!"

Schroeder had been thinking the same thing. Now he had an inspiration. "Yes, it can, Doc! There's one person in this town who can make it."

Doc Jones's eyes flashed and the same thought struck him. "Brandon Thomas!" he said. "Good! You call George Thomas. I'll call Mary and tell her to phone Chip that we're on our way!"

While Schroeder was feverishly pushing phone buttons for George Thomas, Doc Jones was trying to reach Mary Hilton. John Schroeder explained the plan, and

STRIKE THREE!

George wanted to be a part of it right away. "We're coming!" George shouted into the phone. "We'll be at the Sugar Bowl in five minutes!"

"Drat this phone!" Doc growled. "Just when I'm in a hurry for the first time in forty years—Hello, hello! Mary? This is Doc! Tell Chip we're coming. . . . Yeah! Sure! . . . With that crazy Thomas kid. Brandon! Yeah, and old man Thomas too. We'll be there! So long!"

At the sound of Brandon's horn, the two old friends charged into action with Nick Trullo and Ken Carey in tow.

"But, Mr. Schroeder," the cashier cried, "who'll be in charge of the store?"

"Petey!" Schroeder yelled, halfway out the door.

"But his grandmother died—again!"

"Oh, yeah, that's right! Well, close the darn place!"

That was all she heard above the clash of meshing gears and the roar of a racing motor. They were on their way!

All morning, Chip had kept the line between University and Valley Falls jumping. He was the first player out of the bus when the team arrived at the field house. He glanced at the clock on the tower and groaned. "Twelve forty-five. An hour and fifteen minutes to go before warm-ups!" Once more Chip dashed to the phone. After five frantic minutes, Chip got his mother again.

"Yes, Chip, they've left. With Brandon Thomas!"

Chip breathed a sigh of relief. If anyone could do it, Brandon could. *He* ought to know!

Chip hurried down to the locker room and informed Rockwell that Nick was on his way. "No problem, Coach. They'll make it," he said. "Brandon Thomas is driving!"

THE PRODIGAL PITCHER

"That's not very reassuring, Chip!" Rockwell grunted. "I hope they make it—alive."

Chip watched the clock. So did Rockwell. When everyone was dressed, Rockwell called the team together.

"I've decided to reinstate Nick Trullo. He's on his way here, right now."

Rockwell paused and looked around the circle of players' faces as a murmur of protest began. Under his direct glance the players grew silent, and he continued in a sharp, commanding voice. "I believe every player here realizes it is my prerogative to determine the personnel of the squad. I want all of you to know that the fact Nick Trullo is on his way here, now, is sufficient evidence for me that he realizes his mistakes. I expect every player to back him up to the limit if he gets here in time to pitch. All right, now. We can win this game, with or without Nick Trullo, if we hustle. Now, Nick may make it in time to start the game and he may not. We've got to hope that something happens to hold up the starting time.

"But if nothing happens and if Trullo doesn't arrive in time, we'll start this way: Collins, Morris, Williams, Cohen, Hilton at center field, Badger, Rodriguez, Carey, and Schwartz."

Schwartz gulped and shook his head. "But, Coach! I never—"

Rockwell held up his hand. "Stop right there, Schwartz. You're going to pitch, or at least throw the ball to the catcher, whether you like it or not!

"Now, one last word! This is the game we've been pointing to all year. Some of you may never have another chance to play on a state championship team. Certainly, it's your captain's last chance. Let's win this one for Ted!"

STRIKE THREE!

Seventy miles away, a small-town physician was sitting in the back seat of Brandon Thomas's sardine-packed car, dubiously looking at his pocket watch. Doc Jones was disgusted. He nudged the distinguished-looking man next to him. "What's the matter with this thing, George?" he asked gruffly.

"This thing?" George Thomas repeated. "What do you mean?"

"Nothing, except that they'll probably be calling the game on account of darkness by the time we get there. You see that speedometer up there?"

"Yes."

"Well, this thing has been progressing at the incredible speed of almost fifty miles per hour!"

George Thomas leaned over and looked at the speedometer. "What do you know, you're right!" he said. Then he leaned forward and tapped his son on the shoulder. "Brandon, what's the matter with this car? Can't it go any faster?"

Brandon Thomas looked over his shoulder in disgust. "What's the matter?" he repeated bitterly. "Dad, you know what the matter is! You had a governor put on the carburetor so I could do only fifty miles an hour down a steep hill, that's what the matter is!"

George Thomas muttered something under his breath. Then he nearly broke Brandon's eardrums with a roar, "Well, take it off!"

Brandon grinned delightedly and slammed on the brakes. "You got it!" Up went the hood. Down it banged. Away they flew.

"That was mighty fast work!" John Schroeder observed.

"Yeah, wasn't it? I've seen slower Indy 500 and NASCAR pit stops!" Doc Jones chuckled. He nudged George Thomas.

"Your son seems to know a lot about engines. He did that rather easily!"

"Yes, he sure did do it easily," agreed George Thomas, looking at the back of his son's head suspiciously. "A little too easily!" He pulled his hat down a little farther on his head and nudged Jones. "Someone better watch out for one of those state troopers. We don't want to get stopped. Let me know if you see one!"

Some twenty miles and fifteen minutes later, Doc Jones nudged George Thomas. "I found them!" he hollered.

"Found who?"

"The state troopers! They're right behind us!"

They were—one car and one motorcycle! Lights flashing and sirens blaring. Brandon sighed resignedly and pulled the car to the side of the road. Two state troopers approached the car and looked the occupants over carefully and thoroughly.

The tall one removed his sunglasses and regarded Brandon questioningly. "Nice landing, young man! The strip's a little narrow though, isn't it?"

George Thomas leaned forward. "We were going fast, officers," he said in a straightforward manner, "but we were in a hurry!"

"Going to a fire, I suppose," the short officer suggested.

"Or maybe to a ball game," the tall one said understandingly.

"That's absolutely right, officer!" George Thomas agreed emphatically. "That's just where we're going!"

"That's *just* what *you* think!" the tall one growled. "Please follow me!"

The stern man behind the desk was very polite. He was sure he'd heard everything through the years about

STRIKE THREE!

ball games. But he'd never heard of a bunch of grandfathers flying along the highway to get to a game with the prodigal pitcher! Oh, yes, he had frequently read Frank Merriwell books when he was a boy about the star pitcher being kidnapped, even watched a recent HBO movie about the kidnapping of a star NBA basketball player. But he'd never heard of a story quite like this one. This deserved a call to the university!

Some ten minutes later and some $150 lighter, George Thomas and his traveling companions were on their way again, this time with an escort of two officers who were delighted with the opportunity to see a ball game. Acting on the suggestion of the sergeant who had given them the assignment, they thought it would be nice if they could be there for the first inning. The sergeant also figured an escort was safer for everyone on the highway, as well. Brandon was amazed at what two sirens could do to a crowded highway.

CHAPTER 26

The Hidden-Ball Trick

PETEY JACKSON was disgusted! He sat in the dugout next to Paddy and groaned as if in physical pain every time Red Schwartz toed the warm-up rubber and threw the ball. When Red heaved the ball, he teetered on the practice mound like a juggler balancing a broom on the end of his nose.

Petey glanced at the clock and then at the three umpires standing near the bleachers. Then he saw something! Two boxes of baseballs were resting on the bleacher railing behind the umpires. Once again, Petey looked at the clock. Then he snapped his fingers, nudged Paddy, and spent a precious minute whispering something in the little mascot's ear.

Seconds later, Paddy steered Soapy toward the bleachers where the umpires were standing. Just as they reached the group, Petey appeared and, without a word, socked Soapy on the jaw. Then Petey dashed behind the umpires.

STRIKE THREE!

Soapy let out a howl of rage and chased Petey, and the trio of umpires scattered as the two struggled back and forth. "You crazy?" Soapy yelled. "Oh, my thumb! What's the matter with you?"

But Petey didn't intend to stand up and fight. He broke away from Soapy and dodged around the laughing umpires. Rockwell came hustling over to the group. "What's the matter with you two? Cut it out! Soapy, you get back over there in that dugout and stay there! And, Jackson, you get up in the bleachers and stay there."

The three umpires got a big kick out of the incident. They thought it was very funny. Distracted, they continued to laugh at the antics for several minutes. Then, one of the trio glanced at the field house clock. "OK, men," he said. "It's game time! Let's go!"

"Where's the balls?" one of them asked.

"Why, they were right there on the edge of the bleachers a minute ago."

"Well, they're not there now!"

"Well, what d'ya know about that?"

"Do you suppose those kids . . . ?"

"Don't imagine. The teams didn't use them. Somebody in the crowd maybe."

"They've gotta be here! Somebody's playing a joke."

"Well, they're not here! What are we gonna do? We gotta have game balls!"

"Have the announcer go on the P.A. system and say that the game won't start till they're returned!"

For the next ten minutes, the announcer pleaded over the public address system, but the balls did not reappear. Then the head umpire decided to start the game with two of each team's practice baseballs, but Rockwell flatly refused. It was the responsibility of those in charge of the game to provide new, official balls, and he wasn't going to use old ones. He didn't care how long the game was held up! Even as he spoke, Rockwell was watching the gate.

The crowd turned to the blaring sounds of sirens and watched a strange parade entering through the main gate. Two state troopers on motorcycles were leading an obviously overcrowded car. In the back seat, three well-fed, prosperous looking men sat contentedly. In the front seat, sat three young men.

"It's Governor Coats!" someone shouted. "And some of his staff!" Then the spectators were on their feet cheering and yelling. The ushers made a big fuss, too, escorting the three men to special seats in the grandstand. George Thomas thought the reception was just fine. He raised his hand and beamed in all directions. "I didn't think everybody would feel so excited about us doing a little thing like that," he whispered to Doc Jones.

Doc was suspicious. "Something is wrong here!" he kept repeating. "Something is really wrong here!"

Ken Carey and Brandon had scrambled out of the car and rushed Nick to the dugout. Chip, Chet Stewart, and Pop Brown all helped Trullo put on the extra uniform the team always brought along just for an emergency.

When Trullo was dressed, Rockwell sent everyone out of the dugout and sat down beside Nick. The words that passed between those two were never known, but they were seen shaking hands as though they were old friends who hadn't seen each other for years.

While the umpires were waiting for the university equipment manager to return with a new box of balls, little Paddy won the gratitude and applause of everyone at University Field when his sharp eyes located the two lost boxes of baseballs. Someone had tucked them under a corner of the bleachers.

STRIKE THREE!

Rockwell revised his lineup. "This is it. I'm going to hold Chip on the bench for pinch hitting. Some situation is going to come along during this ball game where a pinch hitter on the bench will be worth his weight in gold! Now the batting order: Rodriguez, Collins, Morris, Williams, Cohen, Schwartz, Badger, Carey, and Trullo. Let's get Nick some runs—quick!"

Trullo started out to the warm-up area. But after a few steps, he stopped. "What's the trouble, Nick?" Stewart asked.

"Nothing, I guess."

Chip had noticed Nick's first steps. "It's the shoes," he said. "They're too small. Right, Nick? Here, take mine."

It was the shoes, and they were too small. Chip's shoes fit perfectly although the pitching plate was on the wrong shoe.

"But what about you, Chip?" Trullo asked.

"Never mind me," Chip answered. "I'll be sitting down most of this game." He smiled at a sudden Soapyism: "Pinching shoes shouldn't hurt a pinch hitter!"

Since the Big Reds were first at bat, Nick Trullo had a little extra time to warm up. Chip stood beside him while the powerful left-hander burned pitches to Carl Carey.

"Do you feel all right, Nick?" Chip asked anxiously.

Trullo paused in his windup and turned to face Chip. "Never felt better in my life, Chip," he said, looking straight into Chip's eyes. "Yes," he continued slowly and thoughtfully, "I'm all right. Now! Thanks to you, Chip. I must have been crazy."

Chip slapped him on the back. "Skip it, Nick," he said happily. "We're all glad you're back!"

Nick Trullo was in good form! So was Stretch Holmes, Coreyville's All-State fireball hurler. The game started off like a hurlers' battle and that's what it turned out to be.

THE HIDDEN-BALL TRICK

Inning after inning, in monotonous fashion, Trullo and Holmes set the hitters down in one-two-three order.

In the top of the fifth it looked as though the Big Reds might push a run across. Biggie Cohen led off and pulled a solid double into right field. Red Schwartz laid down a perfect sacrifice bunt that advanced Biggie to third where he could score on almost any kind of hit, and Chris Badger was up. But Holmes had Chris and Carl Carey handcuffed. Chris bounced one straight to the first baseman for an easy out, and Carl went down swinging. Biggie died on third.

Chip had practically worn a hole in the bench as he twisted, turned, and fidgeted with every play. As he sat there in the last half of the fifth, watching Nick take his windup, he remembered Doc Jones's words. He smiled grimly as he muttered them under his breath. It sure was tough to stay on his toes while sitting on the bench.

CHAPTER 27

Strike Three!

NICK TRULLO couldn't believe it! He never dreamed he would fall for that silly drivel about team play and team spirit. Now, for the first time in his life, he actually felt the bond that connects the very heart and soul of a group of athletes playing together for a common cause. He put his heart and every ounce of his physical power into each pitch, and he pitched as he'd never pitched before.

Stretch Holmes was pitching for all he was worth too. Holmes was an experienced pitcher, a senior, and this was his last high school game. He wanted to win that championship for his school and his team too.

The two boys set a killing pace for each other. The pressure was terrific. Every inning the fans expected one of the boys to break. But there was no break—and no breaks; no one scored.

In the top of the eighth, Carl Carey led off with Nick Trullo on deck and Mike Rodriguez in the hole. Carl stepped into the batter's box and crowded the plate. He wanted to get on any way. Carey had a good eye, and he worked Holmes for all he was worth, finally getting a free ticket to first base. Rockwell stopped Nick Trullo as he started for the plate and talked to him. The result was a neat bunt in front of the plate that advanced Carey to second. The catcher threw Nick out by ten feet. It was one down, with Carey on second base.

Mike Rodriguez, on deck, had been swinging three bats. Now he tossed two of them away and stepped into the batter's box. Then he stepped right out again and called time. Turning toward the dugout, he trotted over to Rockwell. "Coach," he said excitedly, "let Chip bat for me! Any kind of hit will score Carl now, and Chip can do it!"

Rockwell studied the nervous little fielder. Then he snapped his fingers. "Now's the time, Mike. Sure, Chip can do it! Chip! Hit for Rodriguez!"

Chip was surprised. It took several seconds for the summons to penetrate. Then he jumped to his feet. Imagine that! Mike taking himself out of a championship game so another player could hit in his place. What a guy!

Paddy raced up with Chip's favorite bat. "You can do it, Chip," he said. "It's right down your alley!"

Chip took the first one. It was a ball. The next was a called strike. Then another ball. On the two-and-one pitch, Chip swung with all his might at what looked like a fastball straight down the middle. But Holmes broke it off right in front of the plate, and the ball spun off the handle of Chip's bat and went bobbing down the first-base line. Chip grunted in disgust but pivoted and ran for first base.

The Coreyville first baseman fielded the ball right in front of the bag and waited for Chip to come to him for the easy out. All the time though, he was watching Carey who had rounded third on the play and gone a little way toward home. But Carl wasn't going to risk an easy out with the precious run he was carrying and stopped a short distance past the bag.

Chip dug on down toward first but, just as he got close to the first baseman, pivoted and started back toward home plate. The crowd roared, and the surprised first baseman started after Chip. Then realizing that Chip was trying to draw a throw, he backpedaled toward the bag. But Chip turned again and this time sprinted toward the first baseman and the bag at full speed.

At the same time, Carl Carey decided to take a chance. He darted for home. Chip stopped inches short of the first baseman, and the frustrated player hurled the ball home. But the throw was high and a split second late, and Carl Carey scored the first run of the game.

It was a run in, one down, and Chip safe on first base as Cody Collins came to bat. Chip glanced at Cody and got the sign for the hit-and-run. He took a short lead and then watched the play develop. Holmes expected it and threw a wide one. But Chip was playing it safe too. He wasn't going until Cody got a piece of the ball. At that, he barely got back in time to beat the catcher's throw to first.

On the next pitch, Cody swung hard and drove a hard grass cutter down the third-base line. The third baseman fielded the ball with his bare hand, gauged second base and Chip's flying figure, and threw to first for the out. Chip hooked into the bag and popped right up to his feet, prepared to go on if the throw to first was bad.

Speed Morris tried to bring Chip in, but Holmes had his number and Speed went down on the fifth pitch for the Coreyville hurler's tenth strikeout. The score: Valley Falls 1, Coreyville 0.

STRIKE THREE!

Coreyville was at bat, and all its supporters were cheering for a rally to tie it up or to go ahead for the championship. Every Big Red was thinking the same thing: only three more outs!

Chip's spirited words boomed in to join those of all the other Big Reds in the field and in the dugout. No one was sitting in the Valley Falls dugout now! Even Rockwell was out in front, kneeling on the ground and adding his voice to the thunder of the teams and the stands.

Nick was tired. And so was Carl Carey. The nervous strain had begun to tell on Carl. His face was drawn and pale even through the perspiration and dust that streaked it. But he never stopped his chatter, his pleading for Nick to "put it in there!"

The hopes of all the Valley Falls fans rose when Nick struck out the Coreyville leadoff man. But then, he walked the number-two batter. Now, the Coreyville power hitters were coming up. The Coreyville coach called time and talked to his number-three hitter.

Chip was beginning to feel the pressure, and he knew Trullo must be twice as stressed. Would the Coreyville coach advance the runner to second and hope his cleanup hitter could bring him in? Would he play for the tying run? Or would he try a steal? The hit-and-run? Or would he hit away?

It wasn't long until Chip found out. The batter met Nick's fastball right on the nose, and the ball sailed over Cody Collins's head toward right center. The runner on first rounded second and headed for third. Red Schwartz came in fast, and Chip and Ted backed him up. It was a good thing they did! The ball took a bad hop and leaped over Red's head. Chip fielded it on the dead run and fired the ball home on a line. There was no chance for a play at third. But Nick cut off the throw and winged the ball back to Cody Collins who tagged the overanxious runner for the second out. But the tying run was on third, and Coreyville's big gun was up. The cleanup hitter!

Nick shook off Carl's signs twice and then blazed his fastball down the middle of the plate. It was a called strike. Then Nick wasted one, a teasing change-up, for a ball. His next pitch was a curve, and it broke just outside, but the Coreyville slugger stepped into it, and the ball shot straight toward the mound, striking Nick on the leg.

The ball was hit so hard and its speed was so blinding that Nick felt the pain before he saw the ball. Then he made a desperate dive, picked the ball up in his gloved right hand, and scooped it toward Carl. The runner from third had started home but darted back when he saw the ball would beat him in.

Trullo was still on the ground clutching his leg when Carl called time and tossed the ball to Biggie Cohen, who had backed up the plate. Rockwell came running onto the field as Nick gamely tried to get on his feet. But he couldn't stand. "I'll walk it off, Coach," he gasped, "in a second or two."

But Nick couldn't walk it off. Doc Jones scrambled out of his special seat in the grandstand and, after one look at the rapidly swelling leg, glanced at Rockwell significantly.

"Looks bad, Rock," the doctor said.

After Nick was stretched out in the dugout and while Doc Jones was working on his leg, Rockwell waved to Chip. Chip's heart jumped. As Chip trotted in to the mound, his feet were cramped by the tight shoes and he wished he had his own spikes with the pitcher's plate on the right shoe. But there wasn't time to think about that now.

STRIKE THREE!

With the umpire's "Play ball," Schwartz moved halfway between center field and right field, and Ted Williams did the same on the other side.

Even though Chip was worried about Nick's ankle and the game, he couldn't resist a grim chuckle. Playing for the state championship with eight men in the infield. What next?

The umpire gave Chip a few extra warm-up pitches and then he was ready. Carl trotted halfway to the mound. "Only three more strikes, Chip. You can do it!"

Chip sized up the tall hitter standing relaxed just outside the batter's box. The hitter looked Chip over too. Then he stepped up to the plate, and Chip waited for Carl's sign.

Carl called for a fastball, and Chip zipped it right down the middle. It was a called strike. Chip breathed a short sigh of relief. At least he was ahead of the hitter for a second or two. Then Carl called for a low one, inside. Chip blazed it in, and it was a ball. A curve and two fastballs, and the count was three and two. Chip reached for the little rosin bag, keeping his eyes on the runner on third all the time. This was it! One run ahead, extra innings, two on, two down, and three and two on the batter. What a spot to be in!

One strike to go and the Big Reds would be state champions. Yes, and one bad pitch and they would be nothing but runners-up. He had to strike this tall guy out! But with what? Chip moved his foot in a half circle from right to left. Then something clicked. The blooper! Taps's blooper!

It was risky though. Carl had never seen that pitch; a passed ball would be as bad as a hit. Then Chip brushed his gloved hand impatiently across his face and called time.

STRIKE THREE!

Carl met him in front of the mound. "What you want to use, Chip? I don't know what to call!"

"I do!" Chip said, rubbing the rosin bag between his fingers. "The blooper!"

"The what?"

"The blooper. You've never seen it, and I've never used it in a game, but the spot's perfect for it, right now! It's just like a knuckler except that it goes higher up in the air. You've got to catch it!"

"I'll catch it!" Carl said fiercely. Then he turned and walked briskly back to the catcher's spot.

Chip watched the little receiver march back to the plate, and his thoughts winged clear away to Valley Falls. *Bet my mom and the people in her department at the office aren't talking right now. They're listening to the radio. Guess about everyone else in Valley Falls is too.*

The umpire called time, and the tall hitter dug in. Chip eyed the runner on third. He figured the tall batter was thinking the fat pitch was coming up now. Well, it was.

Chip was trying to visualize the pitch. How high was he going to throw it? How hard?

There was no thunder from the crowd now. It was as though everyone was holding his breath. Chip gazed at the poised figure on third base waiting for his initial pitching movement. The runner on first had gone on down to second and had already moved far along toward third base, yelling and kicking dust.

Chip wasn't tempted into making a play for anyone but the batter. He shifted his eyes from the third-base runner to the plate and back again to the man on third. Then his arm flashed through in the full swing he used for his fastball, and he lobbed the blooper!

STRIKE THREE!

As in a dream, he followed through and finished in his fielding position. He saw nothing more—neither the ball nor the runner dashing for the plate with the pitch.

"Whoosh!"

The roar from the stands could have smothered the bat cracking the ball or the ball smacking into Carey's big glove. Chip waited grimly, crouched low in front of the mound, arms hanging loose and hands ready. Where was the ball?

Then he saw the batter looking pathetically at his bat and the umpire with his mask in one hand and a hooked thumb held high in the air.

"S-T-R-I-K-E T-H-R-E-E!"

CHAPTER 28

The Team's the Thing!

CHIP FELT as though he were standing on a cloud, as though he were one of those mammoth parade balloons that sway and move so slowly they seem unreal. And then, as in a dream, he saw Carl Carey pushing out of the dust and waving the third-strike ball high in the air.

"You did it, Chip! You *did* it!"

Before Chip could move, Biggie and Speed and Chris and Cody were pounding him on the back and hollering. Despite his struggles and protests, Chip was pushed, tossed, and hugged until he ended up on the shoulders of his cheering teammates. On top of the dugout, for all to see, Pop was dancing, and tumbling out of the dugout came Paddy, hanging on to Soapy with one hand and to Nick Trullo with the other. Nick was hopping along on one leg and yelling at the top of his voice.

Something happened to Chip's eyes then. He closed them tightly and tried to breathe past the overwhelming weight in his chest and the lump in his throat.

THE TEAM'S THE THING!

Suddenly, the feeling vanished—disappeared as completely as the baseball trouble and all his worry about his leg. And, in spite of the yelling and cheering, Chip could hear Doc Jones saying as plainly as if he were right there by his side:

"The team's the thing, Chip. 'One for all and all for one' sounds like idealistic nonsense to a lot of people. But you can't laugh at that philosophy in sports, Chipper. No teamwork, no team! Suppose you just forget about the 'all for one' part and concentrate on the 'one for all.' See that Chip Hilton does what is best for the team. Then everything will come out all right!"

Chip's eyes were clear now. He looked down at the cheering teammates who were holding him, and his eyes met Nick's and Carl's. They were cheering him too. Carl was still holding the ball up in the air and trying to force it into Chip's hand. But Chip pulled his hand away and managed to scramble down from the shoulders of the happy crowd. Then he pushed his way in between Nick and Carl and threw an arm around each of their shoulders.

"Here! Take the ball!" Carl insisted. "You saved the game!"

"Nothing doing!" Chip protested. "It's Nick's! He *won* the game! It's his! What a game!"

"What a team!" Nick and Carl chorused.

As the three boys stood there with locked arms, Chip's thoughts flew to the South Side, to the crowd of South-Siders who had jeered him twice in the past year, to the Hill crowd, to Peck Weaver and Buck Adams, and to Ken Carey and Leroy White. Nick and Carl were members of that crowd.

But a kid had to learn that another guy's thinking and actions were influenced by the people he grew up with, by the life that surrounded him day after day. Just about everybody was all right when a guy got to know him and tried to understand him, tried to look at things from his point of view.

Chip tightened his grip on the shoulders of the two South-Siders. All the worries and trouble had been worthwhile after all! He was glad he had persisted in his efforts to win the friendship of these two. They were really on the team now.

The eyes of the three boys met. They exchanged winks. Then, arm in arm, they turned toward the dugout where Rockwell stood with a happy smile and an out-stretched hand.

■ ■ ■

Summer vacation gives Chip a chance to work a full-time job while playing ten long weeks of summer base-ball. For the first time in his life, Chip comes up against that all-too-common problem—professionalism in amateur sport—and the way Chip handles the situation will make you like this blond-haired teenager more than ever!

Be sure to read *CLUTCH HITTER,* the next Chip Hilton Sports Story filled with sports action and suspense to the final word on the last page!

A Note
to Readers

DEAR CHIP HILTON FAN,

Chip Hilton Sports is dedicated to preserving and extending the legacy of Coach Clair Bee, through the updating of his wonderful twenty-four-volume Chip Hilton Sports series, which has inspired readers for nearly five generations.

Updating the series arose from a promise Randy made Dad shortly before Coach Bee's death in 1983.

Coach wanted new generations to read his series. He hoped they would enjoy and benefit from the positive messages about academics, character, integrity, sportsmanship, and personal accountability woven within the fast-paced sports action.

In addition to the expert sports instruction and great action, the essence of the Chip Hilton Sports series lies in the relationships and sense of community Chip and the

STRIKE THREE!

other characters forge as they experience the joys, challenges, defeats, and triumphs of growing up.

We are starting to hear from you about how much you are enjoying the updated Chip Hilton Sports series. Clair Bee would be delighted that Chip Hilton, his favorite fictional character, is making a hit with another generation of readers! Please visit our website and then write us at www.chiphilton.com.

We welcome you to Valley Falls and State University—the wonderful world Coach Clair Bee created in his Chip Hilton Sports series!

— Randy and Cynthia Bee Farley —
CHIP HILTON SPORTS

*Read what others have to say about
the Chip Hilton Sports Series:*

"Chip Hilton is the kind of scholar-athlete that we want to encourage in the rising generation of young Americans . . . They are stories we need to hear again."
—Senator Dan Coats, Indiana

"The manner that Chip Hilton dealt with adversity and people had a significant influence on my understanding of sports, competition, and life."
—Wally Walker, Seattle Supersonics

"The path to success is never easy, but if Chip Hilton and Valley Falls are any indication of our potential as individuals and as a community, then the journey is certainly worthwhile."
—Michael Clair Farley, UNC at Chapel Hill,
    Class of 1998

A NOTE TO READERS

"In the time I've spent working with young athletes and others, I've continually asked myself, 'Now, what would Chip Hilton do in this situation?' Wrestling with this simple question has on many occasions led me down the road to the right answer."
　　—Chuck Wielgus, Executive Director, USA Swimming

"Through Chip Hilton, Clair Bee positively influenced the youth of America in a bigger way than any before him, or perhaps since."
　　—Dave Gavitt, Basketball Hall of Fame

"I know without a doubt that it was the Chip Hilton series I read as that young boy on the family farm back in Texas that formed my values on how I wanted to compete in sports, but more importantly, how I wanted to live my life as a man."
　　—Mike Hargrove, Manager, Baltimore Orioles

"The Chip Hilton books are ready for another generation. Perhaps they are needed by young people in our society even more than ever before."
　　—Hal Uplinger, Long Island University,
　　　Class of 1951

"For many of us who delved into Clair Bee's books, precious memories abound that last a lifetime. Each book details human qualities for successful living and also teaches us that true champions never quit."
　　—Coach Marlo Termini, Cleveland, Ohio

"Chip Hilton provides great reading and important lessons about the value and values of sports."
　　—Jim Delany, Commissioner, Big Ten Conference

more great releases from the

Chip Hilton Sports Series

by Coach Clair Bee

The sports-loving boy, born out of the imagination of Clair Bee, is back! Clair Bee first began writing the Chip Hilton Series in 1948. During the next twenty years, over two million copies of the series were sold. Written in the tradition of the *Hardy Boys* mysteries, each book in this 23-volume series is a positive–themed tale of human relationships, good sportsmanship, and positive influences— things especially crucial to young boys in the '90s. Through this larger-than-life fictional character, countless young people have been exposed to stories that helped shape their lives.

WELCOME BACK, CHIP HILTON!

TOUCHDOWN PASS - #1	CHAMPIONSHIP BALL - #2	CLUTCH HITTER - #4
0-8054-1686-2	0-8054-1815-6	0-8054-1817-2

available at fine bookstores everywhere